ALL SNOWED GIN

Cover Design by That's the Tits Graphics
Edited by the Happily Editing Anns

1

ROSE

THICK, bright white snowflakes fill my windshield, my hands gripping my steering wheel so tight that my knuckles are white. Yup, that's correct. I'm white-knuckling it.

Given these narrow, winding mountain roads, it only makes sense. The last thing I need is to go slipping and sliding. One good fishtail and that could be the last of me. No thanks. Not what I need. Especially only a few days before Christmas.

"Sorry, Dustin," I say out loud, turning down my stereo so I can see better. Yes, so I can see better. Everyone knows that's how it works. And as much as I love listening to Dustin Wild, hometown boy turned country mega star, croon "Mary Did You Know," now is not the time. I need to concentrate.

It seems the slower I go, however, the harder the snow falls. That shouldn't be how this works, right? Surely, I'm imagining it. I'm also not about to test out that theory either. My happy little lead foot has been retired for the moment. At least until we are back on a main road or it has stopped snowing.

Which can happen at any time. Really. Please.

Until then, I'm going to be thankful for my Jeep. This gal might be as old as I am, but she runs like a dream. Thanks to the world's best mechanic, who just so happens to live in my hometown of Hickory Hills, Georgia, she'll probably run for another ten.

The thought of Hickory Hills sends a pang through me. It's been a month solid on the road—the last two weeks of which were spent in Nashville—wheeling and dealing on behalf of my bosses. Thanks to me, Southern Brothers Brewing will now be featured in fifteen new establishments across the southern United States, including six in Nashville alone. That's on top of Fire Lights, the honky-tonk owned by Dustin Wild, a major attraction for those hitting up Broadway. It was a very successful trip.

One that I thought was going to be topped off by a quick little detour into the mountains. Emphasis on quick. They just looked so pretty as I was driving through Mistletoe Creek, a sleepy little town I pass every time I'm on my way to or from Nashville. That's when the idea hit me. A promo photo of all our bottles in the snow. It was perfect.

At least until the clouds rolled in. And by rolled, I mean rushed. Those babies came out of nowhere. One second it was perfectly sunny and beautiful, a light layer of snow on this rock outcropping I found sparkling in the rays. The next it was gray and overcast, the temperature dropping by the second. Then the snow started.

But it's going to be okay. I can't be that far from the main road at this point. I don't think. Then, I'll be back on my way toward Hickory Hills, and with my family just in time for Christmas.

Pop!

The loud noise echoes through the Jeep, the back end swerving out from underneath me. I white-knuckle it even harder, holding on for dear life. My heart starts to race, and my pulse thrums in my ears. For a split second, I try and remember what to do. Letting up off the gas, I keep the wheel steady, trying to let gravity do its thing. No, not gravity. Gravity would keep me moving—downhill. And since I'm not the Wicked Witch, I am not even going to bother trying to defy that law of physics. Acceleration, that's what I meant.

My Jeep rolls to a stop, my heart still moving much faster than the vehicle was, the crunch of snow underneath it a semi-welcome sound. Once I am confident we're truly at a standstill, I throw it in park and set the parking brake. I don't need the forces in the world to exert payback for mixing them up a moment ago.

I hop out, and a bitter, winter wind hits me instantly, chilling me to my core. Fuck, that's cold! I don't have much more than a heavy sweatshirt with me—I wasn't expecting big-coat weather—but I scramble to grab it from my backseat and put it on. It does little to block the wind, but it's better than exposing my bare arms to the elements. Elements that are flying in my face and making it very tough to see.

"Okay, Blanche," I say, patting my Jeep. I can almost feel her sigh under my touch, her own annoyance with me for the detour palpable. "Tell Mama what's wrong."

Another sigh from her, this one actually audible as the engine makes some kind of release noise, as I round her backside. And there it is.

Staring back at me, almost as if giving me the middle finger, is a flat tire. A fucking flat tire. How does one even get a flat tire in snow? Nothing obvious is poking out from it, and the only thing I can see on the ground is snow. So this is a mystery that might never be solved.

Le sigh.

Nonetheless, it's one I need to fix. And one I can fix. I'm a farm girl at heart, coming from a long line of fruit and nut farmers, so I know how to change a tire. Turning back to my

Jeep, I yank the cover off the spare. Or what I thought was the spare.

"Hell's bells..." I mutter, staring at the tire in front of me. Or what used to be a tire is more accurate.

Stepping closer, I run my hand along the sleek black rubber, my thumb catching on the long, deep gash through the wall. The bright white flakes, still falling at a rapid pace, slip into the grooves of the tire as if mocking me. I get it, universe, it's snowing. And now I'm stranded.

Last I knew, I didn't have cell reception either. I tried to text a picture to my boss, Milo Hayes, before the weather turned, but it wouldn't go through. Something that didn't bother me at the time, but is now crawling under my skin like a chigger. The need to constantly check my phone is probably going to itch just as bad as that damn little insect too.

Great. Just great.

I let out a long, exasperated exhale, my normal optimism starting to fail me. This is the kind of situation that would try anyone. I just need a—

Wait, is that a house?

"Blanche...we might just be in luck!" I exclaim, patting her.

It's hard to fully make out thanks to all this frozen precipitation, but a little ways up the road is a gate. Two tall, brick pillars, each with a flickering light, stand on either side of a long drive, one side of the wrought iron gate wide open. My heart dances, my insides warming with hope. I can't actually see the house from here, but still, there must be one.

"Okay, I'm going to head toward that house and see if I can't call someone about getting you a tire. You wait right here, and I'll be back as soon as I can. Then, the second you're all fixed up, we'll be back on our way to Hickory Hills."

I don't get a response—not that I was really expecting one—so I take off toward the drive. My feet are already freezing, the thin sneakers I'm wearing not doing much to keep out the wet from the snow. But that's okay—because this will all be over soon. As I walk, I let my mind wander, focusing on all the excitement of getting home. Christmas is fast approaching, and the idea that the whole family will be in one place for longer than a meal fuels me as I make the trek.

Before I know it, I reach the house. The massive structure looks like something out of a storybook. Clearly modeled after a log cabin, with classic architecture, beautiful log trusses, and huge windows, it speaks for itself. I'm left in awe of its beauty, especially in the snow, wishing I were stopping here for a long weekend retreat with friends rather than in search of a phone. But that's my main purpose, so here goes nothing.

Lifting the heavy, ornate door knocker, I give it a few taps. The vibrations resound through the wood, the sound still loud, even dampened by the weather. I shiver, my body heat waning thanks to not being on the move, so I take a step back from the door. I bounce up and down, bending at my knees, trying to stay warm. No doubt whoever opens that door is going to think a crazy person has landed at their feet, but right now, not freezing is my priority.

Only, no one comes to the door.

I step back a little more, surveying the house. It's mostly dark, only a faint gleam of light streaming through one window, as if a light is on in a back room. But there is smoke coming from the beautiful river-rock chimney, so someone is home. That's real smoke, as in from a legit, wood-burning fireplace. Not the kind of thing you keep going if you're not going to be home.

So, I do what any sensible person would do. I knock again. And then a third time. I have the knocker raised and ready for a fourth go when the door swings open, knocking me backward. And by backward, I mean flat on my ass. In the snow.

The cold, wet ground seeps through my leggings, my cheeks clenching from the shock of it. Which is also what has me popping back up to my feet in an instant, brushing off my backside. I don't have time to look up though, barely through one swipe at my thighs before I'm greeted with a deep growl.

"What?!"

The voice startles me. It's rough, intense, and clearly not happy. The only thing more shocking than it, though, is what it came from.

And yes, I do mean *what*.

Because the man before me is…more. More what, I have no idea. Just more. Tall, broad, with shoulders that look like he could lift this entire mountain and arms that are thick and muscular. I'm sure those tree trunks he has for thighs are just as overwhelming—and dare I say delicious?—as the rest of him. His dark features give him an air of mystery, the slight graying at his temples betraying his age.

Holy fuuuuck...

"H-h-hi!" I squeak, trying to control myself. Clearly, I'm failing. "I'm Rose Adler. I was driving through and made a detour, then got caught in this storm. And then, I somehow managed to get a flat. Which, you know, really shouldn't be possible in snow. But, here we are!"

Not moving a muscle, he continues to stare at me. I mean, not even a quirk of an eyebrow or tilt of a mouth corner. It's unnerving, but still, I press on.

"Anyway, I don't get phone reception up here, it seems, so I was wondering if I could borrow your phone to call for some assistance."

"Why," he barks. It's not a question, but a statement, rendering me confused. Didn't he just hear me?

"Because I have a flat?"

"How did you get here?"

"I walked up the driveway. I broke down not far from here, or well, not far from the end of the drive, and the gate was open, so I hoofed it up here. I was thinking you probably have a landline, since-"

Bam!

The solid wooden door slams shut, right in my face, once again knocking me back. This time, I manage to stay on my feet. But...did he really...he did, didn't he? He just slammed the door in my face.

What a jackass.

2

PIERCE

FUUUUUUUCK...

So much for my quiet afternoon.

Walking back toward the kitchen, I rub my chest just above my heart. The damn organ is still racing, thanks to the use of the front door knocker. The harsh, heavy sound echoed through the house, startling me. For a moment, I thought I was losing my mind. That I was hearing things. It must have just been a tree coming down outside. Because no one ever uses that knocker.

Then it happened again. And again.

That's when panic set in. Something had to be really wrong for someone to be knocking at my door. No one I know knocks. Hell, no one I know comes to visit. Just the way I like it.

The only exception is my best friend, Lou Meaire. There's no escaping him—trust me, I've tried. But he knows better than to use that knocker. No reason for him to; he just uses his key. Again, just the way I like it.

I let out a sigh, slumping back down in my chair, lifting

my laptop back onto my legs. But I don't get a chance to breathe. Because there's that noise again.

Fucking seriously?!

That girl cannot still be standing out there. Not after I slammed the door. More knocking tells me she is though.

Apparently, she cannot take a hint.

Fuck.

Pushing myself up from my chair again, I storm toward the front door. Anything to make that sound stop. I yank open the door and am greeted with the same sight as before. The most adorable brunette I've ever seen. Shivering.

"What?" I roar, tamping down the niggling feeling that I should be kind. I don't want to be kind. I want to be left alone.

"Hi. I need to use your phone...?"

Her tone rises ever so slightly on the last syllable, leaving me unsure if she is asking or telling me that she needs my phone. I let my eyes scan her up and down. Her chestnut hair is wet, sodden down from the snow, white flakes disappearing into the locks as if by magic. She's in nothing more than a sweatshirt and leggings—both of which are also soaked—and a pair of sneakers that look like they aren't good enough for any kind of activity, much less this weather.

"Let her in, Pierce, she's freezing..." my grandmother's voice echoes in my ear. My insides soften at the familiar voice, wishing it were more than my mind playing tricks on me. Gram is right though. Just like always.

"Fine."

I turn on my heel, not bothering to say anything else. A grand welcome isn't needed. It's not like she's coming over for a dinner party. She's only using the phone. I glance over my shoulder, watching as she struggles to close the solid oak door. She's pushing into it with her whole body, no doubt wondering if it's made of stone, same as I did with a similar door as a child.

When it finally shuts—the distinct click from it latching almost covered by the shuffling of her feet to catch up with me—I pick up the pace. It's time to get this over with.

"Phone's in here," I grumble, nodding toward the kitchen.

"Thank you soooo much," she replies. "I'm sorry to disturb your afternoon, but my phone was having a hard time getting a signal in the storm."

"Cell service is spotty up here. Can't be relied on."

"Oh, gotcha. I guess that makes sense, being so far out of town and all. I guess I..."

She cuts herself off, jaw going slack, only a few steps into the kitchen. I watch as her eyes widen, darting around the room, surveying the state-of-the-art equipment in here. A six-burner gas range sits over dual ovens, both of which are built into marble countertops. The farmhouse sink is to the right, with a fridge large enough to hold a month's worth of food to the left. It's more than I'll ever need, living alone, but it also holds more memories than I can count. Meaning I won't ever change a thing.

Including the corded phone built into the wall. It's the one item in here that isn't fancy and modern.

"It's old, but it works," I tell her, nodding at the faded canary-yellow device and knotted up cord. "'Specially since there's no Internet."

"Thank you."

Her smile is bright, tugging at a string inside me that I didn't know existed. One that needs to disappear. I step out of the kitchen, giving her the privacy to make her call. The skeptic in me thinks maybe I should watch her, make sure she doesn't run off with the silver. The realist in me, though, reminds the skeptic that she's only wearing a sweatshirt in a snowstorm, so there is nowhere for her to put the silver that I don't own.

"Big Ben, this is Rubber Duck!" Lou's voice crackles over the CB radio in the den. I roll my eyes, hating the nicknames he gave us.

"Hi Lou," I answer.

"Your phone's busy, everything okay up there?"

"It's fine. There's a gal using it who blew a tire on the way down the mountain's all."

"Oh man, in this weather? That sucks."

"Yup."

"Well, I hope she's got a change of clothes, because she's gonna be there awhile."

Errr...what?!

"Come again?"

"That's what I was calling to tell you about. Bridge is out. Roof collapsed. You got your groceries, right?"

"Delivered this morning," I answer absentmindedly. My thoughts aren't on my groceries right now. They are one hundred percent on the brunette in my kitchen.

Who is stuck. Here.

Shit.

"Pierce? You hear me?"

"I heard you. Bridge's roof collapsed. They say how long to clear it?"

"No, but I gotta think at least a couple or three days before they even start with the snow, then Chris—"

"Lou..."

"I know, I know. Not your favorite time of year. Well, no one should bother you now, since no one can get to you."

Which means no one can get to her...

"Good news is it shouldn't take long to clear once they can get to it, it's just a matter of—"

"Lou, I gotta go." My voice is rushed, my insides panicking again. Because I can't turn this gal out.

It was one thing to think I could rush her back to her car when it would only be a few hours for the de Baers to get a tire up here for her or tow her back to Gold's Gas and Garage. But now...well, now there isn't a way for them to make it up here. Fuck.

"Gotcha. Well, radio if you need me!"

"Will do."

Lou says goodbye with his equally weird sign-off, giving me a moment to think about things—and how I'm going to handle this. Because the last thing I want is for her to stay. This holiday is bad enough. No need to go making it worse with company. A stranger at that. But I know I can't turn her out. The weather is horrible and she clearly was not prepared for it.

I'm just going to have to suck it up.

Stepping back into the kitchen, I'm just in time to see her spin around, phone pressed to her ear, smile on her face. Damn, is she pretty. Those bright green eyes sparkle under the recessed lights, lips the color of raspberries just begging to be kissed.

"Oh, hi," she says, giving me a little wave. "What's your number here? The guy at the local garage is asking in case he needs to call back on his way up."

"Is that Winston?" I ask. She nods. I reach out for the phone, not saying anything, but she picks up the hint, handing me the receiver. "Winston, Pierce Adams. Hey, just got a call from Lou. Bridge went out?"

"What? Hold on, Pierce," Winston says. There's a long pause with muffled voices on the other end, but then Winston returns. "Yup, Hudson just walked in and said the same thing. Damn, that's bad luck. Tell your gal there that we'll be up there as soon as we can, but it's gonna depend on the bridge, and with Christmas coming—"

"Yeah, I got it. It's not gonna be today. Or tomorrow."

"Dude, you're lucky if it's this week."

Fuck. He's not wrong. Nothing in this town moves quickly. And with both the snow and a holiday, it's going to come to a standstill. To make matters worse, this is something we all saw coming. That old, covered bridge is pretty, with plenty of history, but has also been the victim of budget cuts for years. It's needed a new roof for a long time. I knew I should have done something about it last summer. I was too lost in my own grief though.

"Noted. Just call once you're on your way. We'll be here."

Winston chuckles before hanging up. At least he finds me funny.

It's time to bite the bullet, though, and break it to little miss I-don't-own-a-coat that she's gonna be here for a while.

"What happened?" she asks, worry taking over her face.

"Rose, you did say it was Rose, right?" I ask. Fuck if I forget her name already. Thankfully she nods, brows turning inward. "Well, Rose, I'm Pierce. And you're not going anywhere."

"What do you mean I'm not going anywhere?"

Her shrill voice slices through the air, making me wince. The worry that was on her face is now complete and utter fear, as she starts to back away from me. Shit, that was not the way to word it. Who the hell am I, Freddy Krueger? I'm not about to hold her hostage in my boiler room.

"Nothing like that. Breathe. I'm not a serial killer."

"Pretty sure a serial killer would say that."

Touché.

"You came into my house, remember?"

"To use the phone! And now you won't let me go."

Ugh. I am not handling this well. I need to start over.

"Hi, I'm Pierce Adams. And the reason you're not able to leave is that the bridge is out. The old roof collapsed and is blocking the lanes. You have to wait until they clear it."

"What? No. That can't be," Rose exclaims.

"Well, it is. So I hope you have more than just that to wear."

"No. I mean, yes, I do. I have a whole suitcase. But I can't stay here. I have to get back to Hickory Hills. It's Christmas! I can't spend Christmas here!"

"I promise you no one is more displeased about the idea than I am."

Rose throws me a look, letting me know that my rudeness isn't appreciated. She is clearly in a personal state of emergency, and I am not helping. Not that there is anything to be done.

"There has to be another way. What about the other side of the mountain?"

"Closest town in that direction is an hour away. On a good day. And they don't service this area. It's too far for them, especially with Mistletoe Creek right there."

The expression on Rose's face tells me everything I need to know. My logic has no place here. Heaving a sigh, she spins around, heading back for the front door. I blink, taken aback by her reaction. Where does she think she's going? Did she not hear me?

"What are you doing?" I ask, following her into the hall.

It takes all her strength, but Rose heaves open the door with both hands, a gust of arctic air whooshing in.

"I told you, I can't stay. I have to get back."

"And I told you, the bridge is out. Not to mention, did you forget that you have a flat tire?"

"No."

I catch up with her, only to stop at the landing. I'm not wearing shoes and am not about to step into the snow to chase after some girl. Nope, not happening. She continues on, pushing into the storm.

"Then what are you going to do? Walk?"

"That's exactly what I'm going to do!"

3

ROSE

Truth be told, this was not my brightest idea.

Then again, what else was I going to do? I can't stay here. For so many reasons. Not the least of which is that I'm very clearly not welcome.

Also, it's almost Christmas. I. Have. To. Get. Home.

So here I am, three quarters of the way down this forever long driveway—seriously, was it this long on the way up?—regretting this decision. Because it's freezing. I swear it got colder while I was in the house. How is that even possible?

Because it's a snowstorm, Rose, gosh...

Tightening my grip around myself, I push on. I have to. My Jeep can't be too much farther, and once inside, I can crank the heat. Then I can figure out how I'm going to get my sorry self down a mountain and back into town. In the cold. Without a jacket.

Seriously, I need to start making better life choices.

And thinking warm thoughts.

A roaring fire. The bright summer sun. Driftwood Beach on Jekyll Island. The very grumpy man I just walked out on. I startle, trying to figure out how Pierce wormed his way into my brain. There's no denying he's hot—HAWT—and could probably warm me up quite nicely if I let him. Let's not lie; I'd totally let him. Even with that sourpuss attitude.

He has no place in my thoughts though. No matter how attractive he is. Who slams a door in someone's face like that? Especially with this weather. And then those comments. *You're not going anywhere.* Seriously, how did he expect that my mind was not going to instantly flash to serial killer? Man must not listen to very many true crime podcasts, or hell, watch the news, if he thought that was an acceptable thing to say to a young woman.

Stop. Just stop. Focus on something else. Something other than the man hot enough to melt the panties right off you in a snowstorm. Like how on earth you're going to get down this mountain. In sneakers. With a suitcase.

Maybe I should have stayed inside.

Stopping in my tracks, I suck in a long, deep breath. The cold air burns my lungs, the rest of me shuddering from the new wave of cold. I really need to get to my Jeep. I can see Blanche's outline start to come into view and that warms my heart. My older brother, Cary, has always made fun of me for painting her lime green, but I've never regretted it. In this moment, it feels like the best decision of my life.

When I finally reach her, I almost feel like I can start to relax. Almost. My muscles are too stiff from the walk and the cold to actually ease any of their tension. Soon enough though, once I get inside and get the heat going. I twist the key in the lock—Blanche is old-school like that—but it doesn't budge. Giving it a little more force, I try again, but no. It's stuck. Frozen.

Well, damn.

"C'mon baby," I whisper, rubbing the lock. Hopefully some heat will help.

I twist again, but nothing. Not even a millimeter. Okay,

plan B.

Squatting down partway, I hold my mouth over the lock and huff. This has to be one of the most awkward positions I've ever stood in, and I'm extremely thankful no one is here to witness this. Because there is no way I don't look ridiculous. Still, I continue to huff, tuning out the world around me as I push as much hot air from my lungs as possible.

Beep!

The sudden, shrill noise catches me off guard, making me lose my balance. Arms flailing, feet slipping out from underneath me, I cry out as I fall. My landing isn't graceful, nor is it soft. So much for all this white fluffy stuff bracing my impact.

"Oww!"

I push up to my elbows, my whole body grumbling. But it's my ankle that's screaming. Loud. Who knows what stunning act of acrobatics I did on my way down, but whatever it was resulted in a twisted ankle. Great—that's going to make getting to town a delight.

"Where do you think you're going?" a voice calls out. A deep, gruff voice. One that is making my already semi-melted panties consider disintegrating altogether.

I look to my left and there's Pierce. He's mounted high on a snowmobile, covered head to toe in snow gear, looking down at me. Oh, good for him.

"I told you, I have to get home! I need to find a way off this hill!"

"And I told you, there isn't one."

Pierce pulls a large, black jacket off his lap and tosses it at me. It lands at my feet, and I eye it for a full five seconds before attempting to move. Pushing to my feet isn't an option though, my ankle making it known that it's not going to bear any weight. I stumble, legs going out from under me like Bambi, landing on my ass all over again.

"Here," he says, hopping off his mechanical steed. He reaches for the jacket, wrapping me in it. The fleece lining is soft against my skin, causing me to snuggle into it. "Hurt yourself?"

"It's just a twisted ankle."

"May I?"

Holding out his arm, he silently gestures his intent to lift me. His voice is still gruff, but his russet-brown eyes have softened, making my heart squeeze. Also, the seeking consent? Can't deny the sexiness in that. It steals my words from me, leaving me to only nod. He does the same in return, silently slipping his arms under me and picking me up in a single move. I can feel the heat radiating off him, calling my name, and I have to fight the urge to snuggle into him. This isn't some romantic rescue in a movie.

"Is there anything you need from your car?"

"My...err...umm...suitcase is in the back," I tell him, my words still failing me.

"Keys?"

"The lock is frozen."

"I got it."

He takes my keys and makes quick work of popping the trunk open. Apparently, the answer to unfreezing the lock was a lighter. Good to know. I'll file that away for next time.

My luggage quickly strapped to the back of the snowmobile, he remounts it, cranking the engine. It rumbles underneath me, sending a very pleasurable jolt to my lady bits, which are already standing at attention. Too long on this bad boy, and it's going to be a very different scene.

"Hold on," Pierce tells me.

Hold on, to what?

I don't have time to get my question out. Instead, Pierce

grabs my arms, wrapping them around his torso. Holy hell. I grip tighter, trying to determine where his jacket ends and he begins. Which actually isn't that hard, because underneath this thing, he is solid muscle. Revving the engine again, Pierce doesn't give me any more warning before hitting the gas.

The cold wind whips against my cheeks, the speed of the snowmobile making it that much harsher, so I bury my face in Pierce's back. He tenses up as I do so, but I can't tell if that's because of me or the curve of the drive that we round. I'm going to tell myself it's because of the drive and give myself another thirty seconds of fantasy of being wrapped around this delicious specimen.

Thirty seconds is truly about all I get though. In the blink of an eye, we're pulling into a garage I didn't see when I was up here earlier, which means I have to let go. Bummer.

"We need to get you warm," Pierce says, dismounting. He turns to look at me, his gaze dragging up and down my body, as if he's appraising me.

This time, he doesn't ask for permission. He just grabs me, carrying me into the house as a groom would his bride. I try to pay attention to the layout as he weaves through the house, but he moves too fast for me to focus on much. My skin prickles from the warmth inside the house, and all I can think of is how nice a bath would be.

Pierce deposits me in a large armchair, propping my feet up on a matching ottoman. Giving me another appraising once-over, he curtly nods, letting out a grunt.

"I'm going to bring in your bag. Then warm up some food," he says, both statements so matter-of-fact that it's obvious there is zero room for discussion on the matter. "And then you can tell me where you're so desperate to get to that you felt the need to run away. In a fucking snowstorm."

"That's easy. Home."

4

PIERCE

HOME.

Of course. Of fucking course.

I'm sure that next, she'll tell me that she has to be there in time for Christmas.

I shouldn't be so cynical. I know this. That knowledge doesn't stop it from flowing through my veins like a raft down the Nile.

Trying to tamp down the urge to roll my eyes, I focus on the task at hand—heating up leftover stew. There's exactly enough for two bowls, which I had planned being dinner for tonight and tomorrow. Except now there's two of us. Which means the groceries I had delivered this morning won't go as far as I expected. We'll have to eat small and ration, but it's more than doable. Good thing I ordered extra this week.

The microwave beeps and I carefully remove the bowl, setting it on the small tray. For a split second I question whether or not I should offer up something else, in case Rose doesn't like stew, but looking around, I don't know what that would be. Everything else would require cooking—other than the cereal in the pantry—and she needs to get something warm in her quick. So I need to get back out there.

I suck in a breath, trying to find strength to turn around and walk the ten steps back into the den. Fuck, it's tough. I can already tell by her happy upbeatness that she's the type that loves Christmas, and the realization that she's stuck with a Scrooge like me, instead of her family, is going to break her heart.

And I don't want to fucking break her heart.

I'm also not about to put on a happy face and pretend like everything is holly jolly either. I want nothing to do with the damn holiday. No, less than nothing. If that's even possible.

"I hope stew works," I call out, forcing myself to leave the kitchen.

Rose doesn't reply, and I'm a few steps into the den when I realize why. I freeze, slamming my eyes shut, but it's too late. I've already gotten a more than perfect view of her almost naked form. In nothing but a skimpy pair sleep shorts that barely cover her ass, her damn near perfect breasts stealing the show, Rose lets out a yip, arms flying to cover herself.

"Oh shit, sorry," I mutter, eyes still closed. My dick stirs in my pants, liking what it sees. Because fuck, were her tits stunning.

"No, no. My fault..." she says hurriedly. I can tell by her voice she's just as embarrassed as I am, scurrying sounds filling the air. "I...I...it didn't seem like a good idea to hang out in my wet clothes, so I hopped over to my bag and...well, yeah."

"Yeah."

Awkward silence hangs in the air, both of us seemingly afraid to move. Thankfully Rose makes the first move.

"I'm decent now."

Phew. I slowly open one eye, then the other once I'm sure

she's dressed. The semi I'm now sporting thanks to the unexpected peep show makes it tougher to walk, but I manage, thankful for the tray to use as a distraction. It's not quite the notebook in front of crotch trick from junior high, but close enough.

"Here," I say, clearing my throat and holding the stew out to her awkwardly, like Oliver Twist in reverse.

Smiling politely, she holds up a finger to indicate one moment, then lowers herself into the chair. I force myself not to stare at her chest, the stiff peaks of her nipples poking at the cotton of her T-shirt. Last thing I need is for her to think I'm some kind of pervert.

"Mmmmmm," she moans, taking a bite. "Oh, this is so good. Just what I needed."

"Good."

"Did you make it?"

"Err...yeah."

I follow suit, parking myself on the old, worn-out couch. It's lumpy and uncomfortable as fuck, forcing me to shift so that I'm not sitting unevenly on the threadbare cushions, while also avoiding the springs poking out. This thing had been long overdue for a replacement, but Gramps loved it too much to let it go. And then I became the one who couldn't part with it. Would have been like parting with him all over again.

"Do you like to cook? Your kitchen is amazing."

Rose's voice is sweet and light, warming my insides just as much as the stew. I'm intrigued by her. Want to know everything about her. From what I can tell, she's the kind of person that will tell me too. I just have to find the right questions to get her talking.

"I make do," I answer, trying to deflect. I need to turn this on her. "You?"

"Oh, I love to cook. Well, bake really. I come from a very

long line of fruit and nut farmers—the three Ps to be exact—so those are always in abundance in our house it seems. Even when they're out of season."

"Three Ps?"

"Peaches, Pecans, and Peanuts," she says, a silent "duh!" hanging in the air, punctuated by a giggle that makes my semi even harder.

"Gotcha."

"Yeah, so I love to fool around in the kitchen and create new recipes and ways to use them. It's so much fun. And my new sister-in-law, Tizzy, well, she's not my sister-in-law *yet,* they're not married. And actually, Cary, that's my brother, he still has to propose. But I know it's coming, so, she's my sister-in-law. Anyway, she's a chocolatier. So, we've had a ton of fun playing with chocolate. For Christmas she's going to..."

Rose cuts herself off, her bottom lip starting to tremble. See, I knew once I got her going, information would flow like Niagara Falls. I just wasn't counting on her making herself cry.

"Is that why you're so desperate that you risked frostbite, hypothermia, and a broken ankle? To get back to dipping shit in chocolate?"

My response is snarkier and terser than I intend. There's no hiding that my question is dripping with judgment. Not that I'm trying. Because nothing could be important enough to risk death like that. Especially not dipping fruit in fucking chocolate.

"It's not just about the chocolate!" Rose defends. "It's Christmas. I want to be with my family. It's our first one with Tizzy, and Mom and I have all sorts of plans and surprises to help welcome her into the family. It's going to be epic. Or, at least, it was."

The loud, harsh sigh she emits is enough to tug on any

heartstring. Even ones as short and singed as mine. There's nothing I can do about it though. Until it stops snowing and they fix that bridge, there's no going anywhere.

"That's not worth frostbite." I mean it as a joke, but the scowl it earns me informs me that it doesn't land as intended. Ooops.

"Says the man who slammed the door in my face when I asked to use the phone. And c'mon, you can't be thrilled that being snowed in is your new Christmas plan either."

"This was my Christmas plan."

"To be snowed in?"

"No, but stay in. By myself."

"By yourself? On Christmas? Oh no, Pierce..."

Rose sits up a little more, leaning forward and reaching out, like she'd take my hand if we were closer. Part of me aches for that—to feel her touch and know if it's as comforting as it seems it could be. But a bigger part says no. Letting her in would be a bad idea. I need to keep my distance and just deal with the fact that we're forced to be roommates for the short-term future.

"There must be someone you planned on spending the day with, instead of being all by yourself," she continues.

"It's what I wanted. Besides, I'm not all by myself anymore, now am I?" I gesture toward her.

"Oh, I guess not."

Frowning, she turns back to her stew. We continue to eat in silence for a long while, not making eye contact, nothing but the sounds of the crackling fire and spoons scraping against the bowls to fuel the already thick tension. I try to think of something to say, to get her talking again, but I can't. Everything I think of is going to come out wrong, or potentially lead me to be an ass again. I've done enough of that today.

When we've both finished, I clear our dishes, taking my

time in the kitchen. I'm all but done wiping down the counters for a third time when an idea hits me. Rushing over to the walk-in pantry, I spin around a couple of times, trying to remember what I did with the little bag. I'm not much of a sweets eater, but every now and again I get a craving for a little something. And for just those occasions I keep…aha! There it is. Grabbing the bag, I empty a handful of the candies into my palm and head back toward the living room.

"It's not peaches and pinochle, but…maybe it'll help?" I say, kneeling down in front of Rose.

Opening my hand, I offer up my palm, three perfectly wrapped Hershey Kisses on display. Rose gasps, eyes lighting up, hands flying to cover her mouth, which is turned upward in a smiler bigger than I've seen from her all day.

Mission accomplished, Pierce...see, you're not a complete ass.

"OMG, thank you! They're perfect."

Rose launches forward, wrapping her arms around my neck. Her quick movement catches me off guard, but I react in time. My arms aren't the only thing reacting though. My dick wants in on the action, now fully standing at attention, as I hold on to her, enjoying the feel of her body pressed against mine. To my surprise, Rose doesn't immediately let go. She holds on for a long moment, and I revel in it, not wanting to be the first to pull away.

Eventually, she does let go, but not all the way. Leaning back a bit, she pauses, her face mere inches from mine, our eyes locked on one another. There's power in her gaze, a burning that flashes through me. I don't know this woman. I want nothing to do with her. But my body doesn't seem to care. It has a mind of its own and is making a list of things it wants where she is concerned.

As she catches her bottom lip between her teeth, Rose's irises darken. My heart jumps, my pulse quickening, but the rest of me is not so sure. Is this actually happening? No, she's just confused. We both are. It's been a long fucking day and neither of us knows how to react.

But then, Rose leans in a little. I follow her lead, feeling the pull. It hasn't been that long since I kissed someone, but it's been a long time since it felt like this, and in an instant, I feel like I'm having an out-of-body experience. That doesn't stop me though. I lean in farther. And then, it happens.

Rose yawns.

5

ROSE

WELL, that was unexpected.

Both the yawn, and what it interrupted. The interruption was probably not a bad thing though. Kissing grumpy strangers who have taken you in out of the storm is not high on the Safe Girl 101 list. Actually, I'm pretty sure that's something they directly advise *against* in Safe Girl 101.

I cover my mouth, sure my breath is borderline fierce after that stew, and push myself back into the armchair. I refuse to be embarrassed. Because being embarrassed would mean acknowledging what just happened and well, no. We're not going there.

"Sorry…sleepy. Guess it's probably bedtime," I say, trying my best to sound nonchalant.

I have no idea what time it actually is, but at this point, who cares. Getting into bed sounds fabulous. Hunkering down and putting this day behind me is exactly what I need. I even have a couple of cute Christmas stories all loaded on my Kindle, ready to go.

"Yeah, yeah," Pierce agrees, nodding. "It's been a long day.

I'm sure you're exhausted and want to rest. So…I…errr…I'll go get some linens for you."

He's on his feet, disappearing from the room faster than I can tell him that I'll come with him and help. My ankle still hurts, but not as bad as before, and it can certainly bear weight now. We might be stuck like this for a couple of days, but I don't want him thinking he has to wait on me. That's only going to make this even weirder.

We need to erase the weird. How, I have no idea. Something else to muddle on while I lie in bed.

"Here." Pierce holds up a stack of baby-blue sheets, piled neatly on top of a forest-green fleece blanket. They look soft and clean, making my body suddenly crave the feel of a bed. "These should fit the couch just fine."

Wait…did he just say couch?

"Couch?" My voice croaks, betraying my surprise.

"Where did you think you were going to sleep?"

Where did I think I was going to sleep? Did this man slip something into his dinner and I just not notice? Or maybe there was something in mine and all of this is some wild hallucination. Maybe I'm already asleep, my mind tricking me into thinking that this is real life and the mysteriously sexy grumpopotamus in front of me is implying I'm going to sleep on the couch.

"A bed…"

"I don't have any."

"You don't have any beds? Do you sleep in a hole in the ground? Suspended from the ceiling?"

Actually, that might make sense. I've somehow transported into some alternate universe and Pierce is really a bat. He sleeps in some unique contraption, tethering himself to the open rafters of this house.

Okay, Rose...now you're starting to lose it.

"No, I sleep in a bed. But that's the only one."

One bed. One bed. One. Fucking. Bed. He cannot be serious.

I blink a couple of times. Hard. As if intermittently cutting off the view of him will magically make this make sense. He only has one bed. Like this is some sitcom trying to force a laugh.

"Just one? You live in this whole huge house, and only have one bed?"

"It's just me; why do I need any more?" He furrows his brow at me, as if I just asked the stupidest question ever and he can't believe he had to answer it.

I balk. And here I thought the worst was done for the day. Apparently not.

"I am not sleeping on the couch."

Peering around him, I take a moment to appraise the piece of furniture I just turned down. It is older, the faded floral print way past its prime. The cushions are uneven, probably from years' worth of use, and the armrests are starting to fray. A small coil peeks out from the top corner, making me wonder what else it has in store. And if my tetanus shot is up to date. It is the kind of item that is either perfectly broken in or insanely uncomfortable—with no room in between those two. My guess is the latter. The way Pierce shifted awkwardly on it as we ate only confirmed that suspicion.

"I guess you could sleep in the armchair, if you don't mind sleeping upright."

Don't mind sleeping upright? First tetanus and now this. Not to sound too spoiled, but this man has lost his damn mind.

"I'll take the bed."

"Not much of the sharing kind, darlin'."

Pierce's southern drawl goes from subtle to syrupy thick on the word *darlin'*, kicking my pulse up about three notches.

My lady bits also get in on it, standing at attention, waiting for more. They've gotten me into enough trouble tonight though, putting thoughts of kissing in my head. So here, now, they need to stand down.

"You could take the couch."

"Why would I do that? It's my bed."

"It'd be the gentlemanly thing to do," I point out, feeling impressed with myself for that comeback.

"Not much of a gentleman either," he grumbles, voice lowering, rumbling through me.

Ohhhhhh, fuuuuuck...

Well, it's a good thing I'm no longer wearing panties after that response, because they'd be ruined. Although, these pajama shorts might be sharing that fate.

Stop it, Rose. Focus on the matter at hand—i.e. not sleeping on that couch...

"Well, the couch isn't happening. So I guess you'll have to learn to share."

Pierce glowers at me, growling and dropping the linens on the couch. I smile back at him as brightly as I can, giving him the little sister look that always made Cary give in when we were kids. Only difference, Cary's my brother, and I think sharing DNA means this look had more potency. I also can't threaten Pierce with telling Mom that he won't share, which means this look is the only thing in my arsenal. Damn it.

Without another word, he spins around, stomping off down the hall that leads from the kitchen. I move as fast as I can, following him, assuming this is the way to the bedroom. My bum ankle slows me down a tad, but I manage to keep him in my sights, even as he veers right, disappearing into a dark room.

I feel for a light switch as I enter the room, my hand quickly landing on it and flipping the rocker switch. A large chandelier comes to life, my eyes going wide with the scene in front of me. There's so much to digest, and I don't know where to start. On the far wall to my right is a massive, four-poster, mahogany, king-sized bed, with a beautiful, fluffy comforter. The duvet alone is calling to me, not to mention all the pillows paired with it. On each side of the bed is a matching nightstand, and a long chest of drawers sits on the adjacent wall, directly next to an old-fashioned wardrobe. To my left I see a barn door that is halfway obscuring what I assume is the en suite bathroom.

All of this is nothing, though, compared to the beautiful stone fireplace that is opposite the bed. Already lit with a roaring fire, it gives the room an ambiance that can't be put into words. One of comfort and warmth, a place you can lose yourself and still be safe.

"Oh my God, this is...beautiful," I mutter, stepping inside.

"Thanks." Pierce shrugs, as if it's nothing. Which, to him, I guess it is. It's his bedroom, so he's used to it. Although, I'm not sure I would ever get used to this. "Bathroom is over there."

"Oh! Thanks!"

It takes some doing to limp slowly to the far corner, but I manage, making quick work of readying myself for bed.

"That's your side of the bed; this is mine," he says as I reemerge.

"What?"

I turn to face him, pulling myself away from staring into the fire. It's just so mesmerizing that I can't help it. Man, I'm going to sleep well tonight.

Pierce sighs heavily, clearly annoyed by all of this. Pointing to the bed, he makes himself clear. "My side, your side. Got it?"

"Aye, aye, Captain!"

"Rose..."

"What, do you think I'm going to maul you in your sleep?" I ask, rounding the bed and pulling down the covers. A light lavender scent fills my nostrils, my body aching to climb in.

"The thought had crossed my mind."

"I'm not, I promise."

Pierce nods, following my lead and slipping under the covers. I get comfortable, snuggling into the down pillows, my muscles relaxing. Damn, this feels good. I can feel myself starting to drift as Pierce turns out the light, and I try to let myself lean in to that feeling.

Except, there's something missing.

I can't name what it is. At least not at first. Slowly inhaling, the lavender now mixed with a musky, manly scent, I figure it out.

Pierce.

The feel of his hands on me when I launched myself at him earlier wasn't enough. All it did was leave me craving more. Even with his surly demeanor. Actually, I think that might have only served to up the ante. Because that scowl on his face is oddly attractive.

There's nothing I can do though. This is my side. That's his. Pierce was very clear about that. Still, all it would take is me rolling over. The heat from his body is calling my name, and I know that the feel of his hard body pressed against mine would be the exact thing to lull me to sleep.

Because apparently I have lost my mind.

A stranger is what I need to lull me to sleep? Get real. I need to stop this. Need to count sheep or sing the ABCs or something. I need to get my mind off the fact that I'm sharing a bed with a man I only met a few hours ago. And not be the creepy weirdo who forces uninvited cuddles on him.

Because that's one hundred percent a creepy weirdo thing to do.

Soft snores start up next to me, and I look over to find Pierce fast asleep. Damn, that was quick. Never would have seen that coming, especially since I was the one who yawned. I roll over, facing away from him, hoping that will do the trick.

No dice.

I lie there, wondering if maybe I should move to the couch. This was a bad idea. That's why I can't sleep. If I move out there, this won't be a problem.

I've all but made up my mind, when a large, heavy arm snakes around me, drawing me close. I freeze, waiting for what happens next. But nothing does. Just more soft snores and Pierce's body heat surrounding me, making me sleepy all over again.

There's no fighting it. Not that I want to. Being curled up next to him feels natural, the sleep coming on faster now, tension flowing out of me. Snuggling into him more, I wonder if he knows what he did, or if he's going to wake up and freak out.

But that's tomorrow's problem.

6

PIERCE

Lazily, I open my eyes, stretching out, enjoying the feel of my sheets. I've never understood what it is about your own bed that feels so damn good, but it's undeniable. The gentle lavender scent from Gram's favorite fabric softener is soothing, reaching down deep inside me. The ache from missing her and Gramps makes its way to the surface, settling around my heart. It didn't have far to travel, the suppressed gnawing a new constant this last year.

Lou tells me that it'll lessen with time, but I'm half convinced he's full of shit. Having never lost anyone, he's not exactly speaking from experience. Still, there is a part of me that hopes he's right, because this is not something I want to live with.

The missing them or the guilt. Especially the guilt.

I roll over, trying to snuggle down farther into my pillow and fall back asleep. Judging by the light that's coming through the slats of the window shades, I still have a little while before I need to be up for the opening bell. The days surrounding the end of year holidays are always a weird time for the stock market, most of the world a lot more concerned with priorities that aren't what's going on with Wall Street. Meaning, if I opted to skip today, no one would notice.

And by no one, I mean me. Since I'm my own boss now.

Something is off though. I suck in a deep breath, trying to place whatever this feeling is. This imbalance. Nothing is coming to me though. Maybe it's just the holidays messing with me. That would make sense. I knew it would be a rough week and that no matter what I did, I'd be all up in my own head somehow. This was probably just the start of it.

Then, I hear the humming.

I bolt upright, my heart clamoring against my rib cage, trying to break free. The soft female voice, wafting through the air and making my skin tingle, has all of me on high alert. Mixed in with the humming is a gentle crackle, a sound any Southern boy would know—oil in the skillet. I inhale again, this time slower, letting my nostrils flare, the distinct smell filling them.

Breakfast.

I panic for a split second. Who the fuck is cooking breakfast? Then I remember—Rose. I look to my right, the crumpled sheets reminding me that we shared a bed. Oh fuck. How did I forget that? I race through the events of last night—her getting stuck, the feel of her against me on the snowmobile, the shape of her perfect breasts in that flimsy sleep shirt as she was eating her stew. Most importantly, her refusal to sleep on the couch.

Which, okay, I can understand. I guess. The thing is old and past its prime. Long past. I need to pitch it, but it's one of many items in this house I can't bear to get rid of. Too many good memories attached to it. Plus the reminder that I hadn't gotten around to replacing it for the two most important people in my life before...yeah.

Nonetheless, she could have slept there. Instead, she wound up next to me. Holy shit. Rose isn't the first beautiful stranger I've shared a bed with, but she might be the first that I've had to interact with the next morning in a more than quick, generic, "this was fun" kind of way. She might also be the first one I didn't fuck.

None of that answers the gigantic question running through my head though. Why the fuck is she cooking breakfast?

Throwing off the covers, I leap out of the bed, fueled by nothing but an irrational need for an answer. Who wakes up in a stranger's bed and then makes themselves at home enough to rummage through a kitchen and make a meal? Rose Adler, apparently.

"What the..."

I cut myself off as I round the corner, stopping dead in my tracks. Oblivious to my entrance is Rose, standing at the stove, Gram's cast-iron skillet in front of her, eggs crackling away. She's humming some Christmas tune I recognize but can't name, dancing in place as she pushes the eggs around in the oil. I can see she's still favoring her one ankle, but she's moving much better than she did last night.

Her ass looks good enough to take a bite out of, barely concealed by skimpy little shorts, her muscular legs doing a damn good job at trying to steal the show. I wonder why I didn't notice them last night—oh wait, because her boobs were on display, that's right. My dick twitches thinking about them again, the rest of my body wanting to slide up behind her, pull her close, and kiss her neck.

No, stop. Do not think those thoughts about the woman you are snowed in with. Not cool...

I shake my head, trying to focus on the matter at hand—Rose has taken over my kitchen. And is likely wasting the limited food supply that we have. Sure, I ordered extra since I didn't want to have to deal with another grocery order until after the New Year, but it wasn't enough for two people for that amount of time.

"Hi!" Rose greets, her smile bright as she turns toward me.

That's when I see it. The tie-dyed purple apron with a picture of the Cheshire Cat from Lewis Carroll's novel, surrounded by a strange, almost psychedelic font quoting the feline himself—*Imagination is the only weapon in the war with reality.* Gram's favorite apron.

Forget an irrational need for an answer. I'm past that. The sight of her in that apron pushes me over another edge. And not the amorous one I was teeter-tottering with a second ago. No, this one is something else. This makes me see red.

"Where did you get that?" I ask, teeth gritted.

"Get what?"

"That apron."

"Oh, it was hanging in the pantry. It's adorable. I couldn't resist. I love *Alice in Wonderland.*"

The happiness in her voice grates on me. It shouldn't, but it does. I don't understand how she can be this happy. Or how she can act like she lives here.

"Take it off," I growl, unable to control myself.

"Ummm, that's a weird request for first thing in the morning, of a woman you barely know, but...I guess—"

"Now!"

"Fine!" she sasses, furrowing her brows at me. She doesn't question any more, but slips the apron off, handing it to me. I yank it out of her hands, causing her to jump backward from my aggression. Still, she carries on. "Well, breakfast is almost ready. I was going to bring it to you in bed, but since you're up, I guess I could set the table. If you tell me where it is."

"No. And what do you think you're doing cooking?"

"What do you mean what do I think I'm doing? I'm cooking! I was up and hungry and you made dinner last night, so I thought I'd be nice and return the favor. I don't expect to be waited on hand and foot while I'm here. I'll contribute."

"You're wasting food."

"I am not," she scoffs.

One hand on her jutted-out hip, she looks at me like I'm insane. Or I need to go back to bed. Which might not be a bad idea at the rate we're going this morning.

"You are," I counter, unable to think of anything else. I have no proof, but somehow I just know.

"Four eggs, four slices of toast, and an avocado isn't too much food. Thank you."

Damn it, she has a point.

"We're snowed in, so what we have is what we have. We have to make the most of it."

"I am aware. I was poking around earlier and saw that you have all the things to make my mama's ham and corn chowder, so I was thinking that I could make that for dinner tonight. It makes a bunch, so we'd have at least a couple of lunches or dinners from it. If you don't mind leftovers."

Fuck, she even made a plan. My insides start to calm, my rational side fighting to take over. I still want to be mad though. I can't explain why, but I do. I don't want this to all be okay. Because it's not.

"Whatever."

"Look here, Ebenezer, I'm not thrilled about this either. I told you, I had a whole big Christmas planned. This is not my ideal situation. I'm just trying to make the most of it."

"And if I don't want to make the most of it?"

Rose balks, hand flying to her chest, like she can't believe I dared say that. Truth be told, I can't believe I said it out loud either. If Gram were here, she would have slapped me upside the head for that.

"I suppose you can deal with it however you please."

"Good."

I bark out my response, earning me a jump from Rose. The reaction puts some distance between her and the stove, allowing me an entrance. In one of the most ungentlemanly moves ever, I stomp over to her, grabbing the spatula from her hand, and then turn to the skillet. I swiftly scoop out my two eggs, adding them to one of the plates that is already home to slices of toast and half an avocado. With a huff, I turn to face her, glaring at her directly so she knows exactly how I feel about all this, before storming off.

She calls out something that I can't quite hear, my elevated pulse thrumming through my ears as I try to calm myself. I still can't figure out why her cooking is irritating me so much. But there is only one place I'll find the answer.

A few minutes later, I'm down in the basement, settling in under the garage. A large sliding glass door to my left leads to a walk-out patio, under the massive deck from the main level, letting in the early morning light. Since the house faces west, overlooking Mistletoe Creek, the majority of the light won't hit until this afternoon, turning the sky some of the most exceptional colors you'll ever see. It's why we built the house facing this direction.

Tugging on the chain in the middle of the room, fluorescent bulbs come to life, illuminating the space. Four copper pots gleam, reflecting back the brightness, greeting me in a way only they can. I set my plate down on an empty table, walking over to the first pot, inhaling the distinct scent of alcohol and juniper berries. Instantly, I feel myself calming, the juniper scent growing stronger the closer I get.

It's too early to sample any, to see if the batch I started yesterday turned out as it should, but I trust my process. More than anything, it's copper pot number four that I'm most worried about, still unsure how the pineapple is going to mix. Time will tell.

That is, if I survive being snowed in.

7

ROSE

I HUM "DO You Want to Build a Snowman," trying to carefully form a decent-sized snowball. The thick, fleece-lined ski mittens I found in the garage are way too big for me, but I don't care. They're too warm to give up. Even if they do make trying to form the start of my snowman's midsection rather difficult.

Truthfully, I'm drowning in most of the snow gear that I discovered. I don't know if it belongs to Pierce or someone else, but thanks to him storming off, I made the executive decision to borrow it. I figured that the worst that could happen is that Pierce wouldn't like it and he'd lose his shit again. Wouldn't be the first time in the less than twenty-four hours I've known him.

I couldn't help myself. The sun is shining, making all this newly fallen snow sparkle like glitter inside a snow globe. Looking at it from the big windows in the living room, it was nothing short of irresistible. It was calling to me. Telling me that I had to come out and play.

So I did.

Getting into the garage was easy enough. It was once I

was in there that it took some doing. Filled with all sorts of miscellaneous items, none of which seemed to have any kind of organization to it, the whole space was overwhelming. Finally, after some digging, I found the winter gear to keep me warm on my adventure. An adventure that I desperately needed.

My phone buzzes in my pocket, stealing my attention from my creation. Whipping it out, I remove a mitten, unlocking the screen.

CARY: Glad you're okay. We were worried when we didn't hear. I know the area you're talking about, and yeah, reception is spotty. Keep us as updated as you can

I TAP BACK A THUMBS-UP EMOJI, saying a little prayer it goes through. With barely the smallest bar of cell service up here, it was a miracle that the one I sent my family this morning letting them know I wasn't dead in a ditch went through. I probably should have tried texting last night and not let my mother fret for longer than needed, since I'm sure she didn't bother checking the voicemail I left on her cell. Although, she's the type that will wear a hole in the floor pacing no matter what.

On second thought, I probably should have called Cary from the get-go and let him inform our parents. That would have been the smart thing to do. But I wasn't thinking clearly after the afternoon I'd had and was too worried about having made a long distance call. I was not looking to piss off the beast anymore than I already had.

Layering up again, I continue my craft, now rolling my snowball, working on strengthening the midsection. By the time I get it where I want it, I'm nice and warm, so I don't hesitate getting started on the head. After yesterday, I know how quickly this weather can turn. I continue to hum, switching over to Mariah, Britney, and some of the other more pop-y Christmas tunes as I work, my heart filled with joy. This might not be the Christmas holiday I imagined, but here I am, so I'm going to make the most of it.

"Look at you, sir," I say to my lopsided, three-tiered figure. "Looking decent. Although, you could be a little more dapper. Let me see what I can find to spruce you up."

With a nod, I head back to the garage, certain I can find something in there for the finishing touches. Rummaging through a box, I find some things that will work. They're not Frosty's corncob pipe or button nose, but the old bit of wire will work perfect for a mouth, and the piece of yellow scrap wood will be an excellent nose.

"I'm sure there isn't any coal here yet, since Santa hasn't been by to fill Pierce's stocking with it," I mutter out loud.

"Oh, it's just you."

The sound of Pierce's voice makes me jump. Shit, did he hear me? I whip around, hand over my racing heart, to find him framed by the door to the house. Warm light spilling around him, he looks like an answer to a prayer. As if this were a made-for-TV movie, where the male lead appears right as his love interest is thinking about him. Which, I guess I was. Just not in that way. Although, the longer I look at him like this, the more I am tempted to run over and throw my arms around him. To feel his hard body next to mine, letting his heat surround me.

Just like last night in bed...

"Hi!" I squeak.

"I heard a noise out here and thought a critter or something had worked its way in."

"Nope, just me!"

My voice is a higher pitch than normal, and I have no

doubt that my smile must look guilty as hell. Pierce either doesn't seem to notice or doesn't care, walking toward me, closing the door behind him. He's still in his flannel sleep pants, his faded black tee clinging to his pecs, but most surprising is that he's barefoot. Holy hell, isn't he cold?

"I, ummm, I owe you an apology," he says, stopping right in front of me.

"Pardon?" I'm not sure I heard him properly. I'm pretty sure he said he owes me an apology. Which he does. I just didn't realize men like Pierce recognized that about themselves.

"I owe you an apology. Probably a couple, actually. Definitely for this morning. But also last night. I've been a bit terse."

That's one word for it…

"Don't forget the slamming of the door in my face."

"Yeah," he admits, rubbing the back of his neck. His cheeks are starting to pinken, but I can't tell if it's from the cold or from his embarrassment over his behavior. I'm going to pick the latter. Serves me better. "So, I'm sorry. You didn't deserve any of that. This sucks just as much for you as it does me, and I will try to be better behaved from here on out."

"Thank you."

"You're welcome."

Awkward silence falls between us, the faint sound of rustling trees not enough to overpower it. I'm not sure there is anything left to say, but Pierce doesn't move. He continues to stand there, looking like a lost puppy.

"Do you want to build a snowman?" I ask, being very careful not to sing my question. Undoubtedly Pierce is not familiar enough with animated movies to understand the reference, and I don't need to give him any more reasons to believe I'm a nutter. Randomly asking questions via song would certainly not help that cause.

"Build a snowman?"

"Yeah! Well, he's mostly built, so it's just finishing touches now. But, ohh!! We could build him a wife!"

Pierce narrows his eyes at me, a look that I'm getting used to. I don't think I'll miss these incredulous expressions of his once we've parted ways, but at least now I know to expect them.

"Snowman's wife sounds like it's more your department than mine."

"C'mon, please? It's much easier with two people. It'll be fun. Or do you not do fun?"

"I do fun."

Taking a step back, he looks me up and down, eyes slowly raking over me. My heart jumps, my head whirring with questions about what he's thinking. The heat from his gaze is also making me feel a little fluttery. Okay, a lot fluttery. Because right now, it's more than his eyes that I want on me.

I need to break this up.

"Fun requires shoes though."

He looks down at his feet, as if he's noticing for the first time that he's not wearing shoes. This man seriously confuses me. Nodding, I turn back to the box, when something catches the corner of my eye. I stare at it for a moment, wondering. Until inspiration hits.

"Sledding!"

"With the snowman?" Pierce asks.

"No," I giggle. "Us. Me. We can use this."

I point to the kayak, giddy inside over this idea. It'll take some effort, maybe even a good running head start, but it should work.

"You have the slope off the left of the drive. That's perfect to sled on."

"I thought you were from Georgia. How do you know about sledding?"

"We went up to the mountains a few times when I was little. Sledding was my favorite."

Pierce simply nods, not budging from his curmudgeonly stance. Fine. He doesn't want to have fun; I'll go without him. I give him my brightest smile and take off at a run, kayak in hand. I can't move very fast since all these clothes are too big, but I still manage to get a decent approach to the hill.

Loading myself as much into the kayak as I can, I move my hips, inching the boat forward. It takes a long moment, but just as I thought, it works. With a tip of the front, I go speeding down the hill. My cheeks tremble in the cold air, my smile as big as possible. My heart is light and happy, pure joy taking over. At least until I slow down, the landscape flattening out. Popping up to my feet, I giggle, unable to hold back, and I climb the hill, dragging the kayak behind me. I'm ready to go again, until I see something that stops me in my tracks.

Pierce. Decked out in his snow gear. Holding a sled. An actual sled.

"OMG! Where did you find that?"

"About six feet from where you found the kayak."

I giggle. Good call. I guess I could have looked closer. I can feel my smile growing again, my pulse speeding up. A real sled. I haven't been on one of those since I was little.

"Shall we?" Pierce asks, holding up the sled.

"Yes!"

I grab his hand, leading him over to the hill. We get ourselves situated, the wood slats colder than expected underneath me. That is, until Pierce scoots in closer, wrapping both his arms and legs around me, resting his feet on the metal bar out front. I rest my back against him, inhaling his distinct, manly scent.

"Ready?" he asks, grabbing ahold of the steering string.

"Let's go!"

"Hold on!"

I wrap my arms around his legs as he moves us forward, gyrating his hips much like I had in the kayak. Feeling him do that against me is a lot more fun than I had in the plastic boat, however. He also accomplishes it much faster than I did, sending us hurtling down the hill. We're moving faster than I did on my solo run, and I shriek, loving the speed. I hold on to Pierce tighter, his own laughter ringing out into the air.

If I thought my heart felt light before, I was wrong. It's nothing compared to what I'm feeling now. This is perfection. And I never want this moment to end.

Except, that's not how this works.

As we reach the leveling off point, Pierce tries to steer the sled, turning us. He pulls too much on one side though, and the sled fishtails, sending us both toppling over. I land with an *ooff*, right on top of Pierce.

Who is thankfully still laughing.

I laugh too, taking a moment to enjoy his smile and how bright his brown eyes are. He's already sexy when he's grumpy and brooding, but this happy version? It's almost too much to handle. Even more so when he wraps an arm around me, holding me close against him.

"You okay?"

"Never better."

"Good to hear."

"So is your laugh."

Pierce laughs more, as if on cue. It's not though. This is deep, genuine happiness. Which makes me even happier. I stare into his eyes, getting lost there, watching them warm up. Each second that passes, I'm drawn into them even more. Leaning in, I pause, knowing what I want but not quite sure if I should. My heart says yes. My body is screaming to just do it. But my head says to let him.

Pierce closes the gap, until we're a whisper away from each other. If I had to guess, his heart, body, and mind are waging a similar battle to mine. I tighten my grip on his arms, hoping that it sends the signal to proceed. That he speaks the same nonverbal language I do.

He does.

In a heartbeat, Pierce's lips are pressed against mine. They're soft, strong, and warm—everything I imagined they would be. He kisses me slowly to start, deepening it as he goes. Each new movement makes me melt a little more. Leaves me wanting more. Head spinning, heart jackhammering against my chest, I give in. This is the kind of kiss that ruins a girl. That leaves you feeling drunk when you haven't had a drop of alcohol in days. And I'm here for it.

A long, drawn-out moment later, we reluctantly pull back, both of us needing to catch our breath. But holy shit, can Pierce kiss.

He smirks at me, giving me a wink. "Wanna go again?"

"Depends. Will every run end like this?"

"Preferably."

"Then hell yes."

8

PIERCE

Pops and crackles fill the air from the freshly stoked fire, the late afternoon sun streaming in through the large living room windows. My body is tired and sore from all the trips up and down the side hill we made, but it was worth it. Rose's bright smile and the sound of her giggle ringing through the air was magical. Not to mention the kiss every time I jerked us off the sled at the end of the run. That hadn't been intentional the first time—simply me being very out of practice on stopping. But it quickly became intentional based on the reaction it got.

Hell, for her kisses, I'd do pretty much anything right now.

Rose saunters into the living room, holding two very full mugs of hot cocoa. She insisted on making some when we finally ran out of steam on the sledding adventure, telling me how it would be the perfect way to warm up by the fire. Handing me one of the mugs, she levels me with her smile, making my already hard dick twitch. I've been sporting a hard-on since the second she wiggled that luscious ass into me on the sled. Proof positive that she's dangerous—giving me a boner while sledding of all things.

I take a long sip of the hot cocoa, watching as she settles into the armchair I put her in last night, admiring how cute she looks. She's back in her normal clothes—sweatpants and a Southern Brothers Brewing T-shirt—and it's taking everything I have not to walk over there, drop to my knees, and devour her. Trying to push that thought out of my head, I sit back on the couch, one of the wayward springs poking me right above my kidney.

No wonder Rose didn't want to sleep on this thing last night...

"Thank you for sledding with me. I had a blast."

"I haven't been in years, and I'd forgotten how much fun it is," I admit.

"Oh, if I lived up here, I'd be going every time it snowed. We didn't take a lot of vacations when I was little—farming is kind of a year-round gig—but when we did, it was around Christmas, since things are a little calmer. No active crops in December." She giggles again and I swear the lights flicker from all her extra energy.

"On your fruit and nut farm?" I ask, as if I know anything about them, which I don't. The closest I've been to a farm is a farmers' market.

"It's not ours; we just run it." The look on her face says that should be obvious, but she's lost me. Which thankfully, she picks up on. "The Adlers have worked for the Hayes family for three generations now. My brother, Cary, is actually Chief Horticulturist—so big farmer in charge. But Daddy and Granddaddy have been helping run the show for years. They all take great pride in growing the best Georgia has to offer."

"Hayes...as in the gun company?" I know the name. I've traded their stock for years. It's a healthy one to invest in, generally providing decent returns.

"That's part of what they do. How they got their start actually. The original Hayes brothers built guns for the Civil War. But now, they're a massive company who, on top of guns and ammo, have divisions for agriculture, paper, and personal safety. One of the Hayes kids also owns The Booby Trap, which is the local bait and tackle shop, and then Milo, my boss, owns Southern Brothers Brewing. All headquartered in our little town of Hickory Hills, Georgia."

"Can't be that small of a town if they do all that."

"Number one employer in Knox county. We joke that either you work for Hayes, or at a business supporting those that work for Hayes."

"Ahhhh."

"What about you?" Rose asks, not letting the conversation lag. "Did you grow up here?"

I pause, trying to figure out how I want to answer. I don't want to lie—and I won't—but how much detail do I want to go into? Looking at her, my heart softens. I want to keep talking to her, and more than that, I want more of those kisses. So maybe it's time to reciprocate the sharing.

"Not in this house. But in Mistletoe Creek, yeah."

"When did you move in here?"

I suck in a deep breath, trying to prepare myself to answer. I know her inquiry is simple curiosity and a desire for us to get to know each other, but that doesn't make it easier.

"Last spring. After my grandparents died."

"Oh gosh!" She lurches forward in the chair. "I'm so sorry. Was this their house?"

"Yeah. It was their dream home." I smile, memories flooding back. I can feel myself choking up, all the emotion I've tamped down for so long trying to make its way to the surface. Inhaling long and hard, like I'm taking a drag of a cigarette, I exhale even slower, giving myself a moment.

"They talked about wanting to move up here for years. That this is where they wanted to live out their days, in a quiet mountain spot overlooking the town they loved so much. So, a couple of Christmases ago, I surprised them with a custom-built house. Found a builder who specialized in mountain cabins and told him to build them what they wanted. He did. They moved in last year, just before Christmas. Then died in February."

Rose gasps, her eyes watery as if she's fighting back her own tears. This was not the mood I'd been hoping for post sledding.

"Parents?"

"Not since I was three. I was raised by Gram and Gramps."

I haven't even finished my sentence and Rose is launching herself at me. I manage to catch her with one arm, without spilling any of my hot drink, her arms flying around my neck and squeezing. Every part of me melts from the feel of her against me, wanting to hold her tighter. Damn drink.

She murmurs something against my neck, her warm breath tickling my skin. I can't make out a word of what she says, so I just nod.

"I'm so sorry," she whispers, pulling back.

"You're not responsible for either of the car accidents that killed them, so..."

"Doesn't mean my heart doesn't hurt for you. I miss my family when I go out of town; I can't imagine having them stolen from me like that."

Stolen. That they were.

But it's time for a change of subject.

"Do you like classic movies?" I ask, hoping it's not too much of a subject change.

"We are Cary Grant Adler and Rose Hobart Adler, so...we were kinda raised on them." She giggles.

My dick twitches again, loving that noise. It's an aphrodisiac all on its own.

"So no Cary Grant flicks?"

"Oh no, I love him. *Charade* is my favorite."

"*Charade* coming right up."

Rose reels back, her face scrunched in confusion. I just laugh, pulling my phone out from my pocket. I tap it a few times, dimming the lights and making a projector screen descend from the ceiling. Rose gasps, grabbing my arm in excitement.

"It's a smart house!"

"It won't talk back. But there's plenty of bells and whistles." I continue to tap at my phone, pulling up her movie of choice.

"We're gonna need popcorn!"

She leaps off the couch, heading toward the kitchen. A few minutes later she returns, Gram's large purple bowl in hand, filled with the buttery snack. I shake my head and she plops back down, snuggling into me. It's the same bowl Gram used for the same purpose. Almost like Gram led her right to it.

I start the movie, putting my arm around Rose and pulling her closer. I don't bother with the awkward first date move of pretending to stretch—we're past that. Which in itself seems weird, since she only showed up on my door yesterday. I can't explain it, but I somehow feel close to her. Perhaps opening up to her was the right move.

The movie plays on, Rose reciting almost the whole thing line by line. I love that she doesn't hold back, letting her real self shine. I love it even more that she jumps a tad every time Audrey Hepburn shrieks. Which, in this movie, is a bunch. I take the opportunity to tighten my grip on her each time, saying a little prayer she doesn't start to pull away.

Thankfully, she doesn't.

At least until the movie ends, when she shifts in my arms to look up at me. "I don't want to move."

"Then we don't have to."

"Good. Want to know what I do want to do?"

It's a trick question, there's no doubt. So I take a moment to try and come up with some kind of smart-ass answer. Only, I can't. So I go with a classic.

"Of course."

"This."

Slipping a hand behind my neck, Rose pulls me closer, gently placing her lips on mine. Her moves are tentative, borderline shy, like she isn't sure she should have been so bold. That needs correcting.

I haul her into my lap, deepening the kiss as I go. I want her. And I want her to know that I want her. She whimpers into our kiss, running her hands through my hair, and mine find her ass, squeezing. Her touch lights a fire in me, her sweet kisses stealing all my attention. Her taste is the only thing I can focus on, wanting to commit it to memory. To never lose the lingering scent of lilacs from her hair. My dick surges, wanting in on the action, but I can't go there. Not yet at least.

We continue to grope at each other, our mouths fused together as we make out like we're back in high school. I have zero intention of breaking this, too caught up in whatever spell she's cast on me to care. If anything, I want more. I want to make her feel good, to make her get lost in whatever this weird pull is.

Slowly, I move my hands up, slipping them under the hem of her shirt. Soft skin greets me, calling me to continue my journey north. Rose moans again and my hands round her front, my thumb grazing just underneath her bra. Her hips move, forming small circles in my lap, undoubtedly coming into contact with my raging hard-on.

I buck upward, letting her know that I want more of this friction.

"Pierce," she mumbles into the kiss.

"Hmmmm?" I ask, my hand taking hold of her breast.

"Let me help you with that."

Rose breaks our kiss, my mouth suddenly missing hers. Leaning back just enough to give me a view of her now swollen lips, she reaches down, grabbing her shirt and pulling it over her head. My eyes immediately fly to her chest, a pale pink bra cradling her perfect tits. I've never once been jealous of fabric before, but in this moment, I am. That only lasts a second though, as Rose reaches behind her and rids herself of the undergarment.

Holy shit.

The most glorious pair of tits I have ever seen are right at eye level, begging to be played with. Rose circles her hips against me again, her core sending a jolt through me. I can't hold back any longer.

I let out a growl, my inner animal unable to control himself. I need her. Need to make her scream my name.

I pull her back in to me, but instead of kissing her, I capture her breast in my mouth, tongue circling her nipple. A small, sharp noise escapes from Rose as I do this, telling me I'm on the right path. I dial in my focus, sucking, nibbling, laving at her, making sure my hand on her other boob mimics my movements. Her coos and keens continue, providing me with a guide to what she does and doesn't like.

"Yes, oh…shit…" she pants, her hips moving faster now, seeking something more.

Something I have every intention of giving her.

Shifting slightly, I free up one hand enough to snake it in between us, slipping it past the elastic of her sweats. The lace of her panties feels course against my overheated skin, but I ignore it, pushing past toward what I really want.

Oh, holy shit...

Smooth skin greets me, easing my way even more. Rose moans, her head thrown back in pleasure, as my fingers slip into her folds. She's so wet, her clit swollen and begging for attention. Feeling the evidence of her arousal turns me on even more, upping my determination. I need to turn her whimpers into screams.

Circling her clit, gathering her wetness, I tease her for a moment. I keep my movements slow, deliberate, wanting to make sure she enjoys every last nanosecond. We're not in any rush. We have all night for this. All night to make her feel like she's the sexiest woman alive. Which, from my vantage point, she is. Continuing like this, I debate my next move.

"Pierce!"

The ferocity in Rose's voice answers my question. It's time for more.

Repositioning my hand, I move to her other nipple, already a taut peak from my attention. That earns me another moan, and enough distraction to slide two fingers inside her, my thumb pressing down on her clit.

"Fuuuck!" she screams, digging her nails into my shoulder.

She bucks against my hands, my fingers slowly moving inside her. I can already feel her pussy starting to spasm, and I know it won't be long. She's so ready, and I can't wait to watch her fall apart in my arms. Picking up the pace, I pump my fingers hard, searching for the secret spot inside her. The one that is going to get her where I want her. I find it, pulling back from her tits so I can watch her face. Giving it a little tap, I thrust my hips upward. Her eyes go wide, then slam shut, mouth open, silently screaming.

Her pussy clenches down on me as Rose digs her nails farther into me. I don't let up though. If anything I pick up my pace, making sure to hit that spot each time. Rose finds her voice, her screams now audible as her body convulses and flushes.

"Oh...faaaa...Pierce!"

There it is. There's my name on her lips. I fucking love it.

It's another minute before Rose comes down from her climax, slumping against me. She's radiating heat like a sauna, her breathing heavy, chest heaving against mine. I wrap my arms around her, holding her close, silently letting her know I've got her. And that I don't plan on letting go.

At least not tonight.

9

ROSE

I PAD INTO THE KITCHEN, rubbing the sleep out of my eyes. The time on the oven clock is much later than my body feels it should be, most of the morning already gone. I can't believe I slept this late. Then again, yesterday was a big day.

An afternoon full of sledding and playing in the snow was more than enough to tire me out. But add in a movie, snuggles, and orgasms? I was done for.

And yes, I do mean orgasms—plural—since what started on the couch was just the beginning. It took a long moment to recover from the earth-shattering pleasure that had ripped through my body thanks to Pierce. It also left me wanting more. The rest of the night was filled with a quick dinner that we flirted and kissed our way through before moving to the bedroom for another movie—that we missed most of, since neither of us were able to keep our hands to ourselves.

Looking around the kitchen, I'm disappointed not to find Pierce. Rolling over and finding his side of the bed cold alerted me that he'd been up for a while. But where did he go? I grab a slice of bread, not bothering to toast it, nibbling on it as I wander through the house.

This place is massive, and I haven't done much exploring. Wandering down the hall, I find a series of rooms, all of which I assume were intended to be bedrooms. Just as Pierce had said, each one is empty, nothing but the beautiful hardwood floors and light from the floor-to-ceiling windows filling them. My heart squeezes, emotion swelling inside me as I mentally decorate each one of the rooms. A massive king-size bed in the one at the end of the hall, with rich jewel-toned linens. Matching sets of bunk beds in the room next to the hall bath, with a mural of a hiker climbing a mountain on one of the walls. I continue on, dreaming up what I would do with each one, until I reach the first one I passed.

I stop, leaning against the doorjamb, wondering how I missed this when I walked by the first time. Unlike the others, this one isn't empty. A large, heavy-looking desk made from a dark wood sits facing the windows that look out over the back of the house, tall trees filling the view. There's a laptop placed on one side of the desk, a legal-size note pad on the other, and in the middle are four computer monitors—two of them mounted to a metal arm above the other two—each one the size of a small TV. All four are switched off, leaving me to guess what they're used for. I didn't take Pierce for a gamer, but what else could he need four screens for?

"Morning."

I jump, Pierce's deep voice both startling and sending shivers down my spine. Memories of him whispering my name, paired with the fantasies I had while I slept about all the naughty things I want him to say to me, take over for a split second. But then I remember what he caught me doing.

"I wasn't snooping, I promise!"

Pierce laughs. "There's nothing for you to find. I wasn't lying when I told you this place was empty."

"I noticed. But..." I cut myself off, unsure if I want to continue. We've found such a nice balance since yesterday, and I don't want to go back to the grumpy version of the man I found when I got here.

"But..."

"There's all that stuff in the garage. Certainly you could bring some of it in? Make this place...homier?"

"Most of what's in the garage is knickknacks and such. Not actual furniture. Most of the furniture that Gram and Gramps had in the old house was, well, old. So, it didn't make the move over. I told them I would furnish the new house too, but Gram insisted that I be there to pick it out with her. She wanted to go right after Christmas, but I had a big thing going on in London for work, so I kept pushing it back. Finally, I told them to just go, pick something out, and they could show it off to me when I got back. That's where they were headed when it happened."

My stomach drops, my heart breaking at his story. No wonder he hasn't made an effort to make this place a home.

"So that's why the couch is...in the state it's in?"

"Yeah. Gramps loved that thing, and I just can't bring myself to get rid of it yet."

"That's more than fair. If I were you, I'd be the same way."

Pierce smiles, his dark eyes soft with emotion. Reaching out, I take his hand, giving it a squeeze in hopes that it will comfort him. He squeezes back, making the butterflies in my tummy come alive. I can't explain it, but I feel drawn to him. There's a connection between us, one that goes beyond us being stuck together for a few days. I just hope he feels the same thing I do.

Because this is going to be super awkward if it's all in my head.

"You'd also turn away from everything and everyone in your life and become a recluse?" he says with a wry laugh. I can tell he wants it to come off as a joke, but it doesn't quite land.

"Maybe not full-on recluse," I admit. "But, I'd hold on to things that meant something. I think it's natural. My brother Cary lost his dog, Riley, last summer and he still keeps her leash in his truck. I took her collar and put it in a shadow box that he now has up in his office. Everyone has something. For you, it's a couch. And, I'd guess based on your reaction yesterday morning, a tie-dyed purple apron with a storybook character on it."

"We're all a little mad here..."

I burst into laughter, unable to control myself. Pierce's dry sense of humor seems to come out of nowhere, catching me off guard. I would love to introduce him to Cary. The two of them would get on like a house on fire.

"Had I known, I wouldn't have—"

He cuts me off with a kiss, my thoughts disappearing in an instant. My knees wobble slightly as I melt into him, grabbing ahold of the side of his T-shirt. Fuck, does he taste good. Like spearmint and coffee—two thing that don't seem like they mix, yet I can't get enough.

Breaking the kiss, he presses his forehead to mine, our exhales commingling as we try to catch our breath. I don't loosen my grip though, still not wanting to let go.

"Wanna see something a lot cooler than my office?"

"Sure, but can I ask one thing first?"

"Okay..." His voice is cautious, like he's nervous about where I might take this.

"Four screens?"

Pierce laughs again, leaning back, relief all over his face. "I'm a stockbroker. I need the different screens to keep up with all the trades being made."

Stockbroker. That makes so much more sense. I knew he couldn't be a gamer—he just doesn't give off that vibe. That also explains how he could afford to build his grandparents such a nice house and then furnish it. Apparently Pierce is not hurting in that area of life.

"Gotcha. But wait—and forgive my ignorance here—but like, don't you have to be, like, on Wall Street for that?"

"Yes and no. I used to be up in New York. Then I was in London. Then everything happened and I holed myself up here. I think it's obvious by now I didn't handle their deaths well. I handed in my resignation, but I'm rather good at what I do, so my bosses said I could work out of here."

I nod, not sure how to respond. Pierce must sense this, not giving me time to flounder but taking my hands again and leading me back into the living room.

"Follow me."

I do as I'm told, not letting go of his hand. It's warm, comforting, and making my insides do a dance. If there was a way to stay like this forever, I think I might. He slows his pace as we reach a set of stairs, carefully descending one by one, until we're in the basement. Thanks to a large set of doors, even this space feels light and airy, and not dank like the basement in the house I grew up in. Turning the corner, my eyes go wide.

A large table runs the length of the wall, a distinct, but telling setup laid out in front of me. Inhaling, my nostrils fill with a familiar scent that I'd know anywhere. Alcohol.

"Stills!" I exclaim. "And they're copper, so it must be gin."

"Wow," Pierce says, taken aback. He looks at me quizzically, but the smile tugging at his lips tells me he's intrigued. "That's...impressive."

"I work for a brewing company, remember?"

I can see the light go on for him. He nods. "Right, Southern Brothers."

"Yup. All the brewing is done in Hickory Hills. Milo Hayes and his best friend, Brandt Rawlins, who run Southern

Brothers together, actually went all the way to Colorado State University and got degrees in fermentation science and chemistry before starting it up. Officially it's just beer that they brew. But everyone in town knows that Brandt messes with moonshine on the side."

"So then this is not nearly as cool as I was hoping."

Disappointment takes over Pierce's expression, and he drops my hand. Oh shit. No. That is the last thing I want him to think. More than anything, I want to hear all about what he's distilling. I have to save this.

"Sure it is! We don't make gin. So all I know about it is that it requires copper pots and juniper berries."

I walk over to the still, peering around each one, as if I have any idea what I am looking at. Truth be told, I don't understand how the beer stuff works either, other than the basics that Milo tells me. All that matters to me is that the end result is yummy, making it easy to sell.

"There's a little more to it than that," he assures me.

"Then I want to hear all about it. And why gin."

"That's easy. Gramps. He loved a good 'Gin Mule,' as he called them. Which was basically a Moscow Mule with gin instead of vodka. When he retired a few years back, he needed something to do to keep him out from under Gram's feet. So, he decided to learn how to make his own. He used to call and tell me all about it and the different things he was trying. When I'd come to visit, we'd spend hours playing around with it."

"Awww, I love that."

"He was a great man. I miss him. But, when I'm down here, with the stills, sometimes I think I can feel him with me."

I turn to face Pierce, my heart ready to explode. "I have no doubt that he's with you. Especially down here."

"Thanks."

"What do you do with it?"

"Drink it, mostly. I share sometimes with my buddy Lou. Sent a bunch to coworkers for Christmas."

"So you have some we can try? This Gin Mule thing sounds fun."

"Sure, if you wanna grab a bottle, there's a wine cellar on the other side of that sliding door," he says, pointing to a large, dark brown barn door to my right. I open the door with a heave, stepping into the dark room. "Just be careful of the—"

"Ahh!"

Pierce doesn't get to finish his sentence. I find exactly what I'm supposed to watch out for soon enough, tripping over something on the floor and into what feels like a large bucket, filled with...I don't even know. It's cold, sticky, and wet. And all over me. At least I assume it is, because I can't see a thing, thanks to the darkness of the room.

Rushing over, Pierce holds up his phone, flashlight turned on. I look down, finding the vat of smashed blue-ish berries turned on its side, the contents strewn around me and, as I thought, on me. Well, I found the juniper berries. And by the looks and smell of them, the used ones.

"Careful of the juniper mash," Pierce finishes, trying to hold back a laugh.

The sound makes the butterflies take flight again though. I know I look a mess, but the last time I landed on my ass like this in front of Pierce, it wasn't laughter it resulted in. I'll take juniper mash over the snow any day if I get to see his smile.

"Don't worry, I found it."

"I see that."

We laugh some more, Pierce helping me to my feet. We make quick work of scooping up the mess, most of it thankfully landing on the tarp that I tripped on.

"I'm gonna need a shower before we get into those mules," I tell Pierce, brushing a piece of juniper-soaked hair from my face.

"Sound like a good idea," he replies, eyes going dark. He steps into me, hands landing on my hips. My body heats up, and I have to stop myself from climbing up this tall, dark, and delicious man. "Want some company?"

Yes, please...

10

PIERCE

"How about I get you dirtier before we get you clean?"

Rose comes to a halt in the middle of the master bathroom, her muscles tensing, a visible shiver running through her. Her deep inhale is loud and stuttered, telling me everything I need to know. She likes the idea.

Coming up behind her, I slide my arms around her and tug her close. She smells of juniper, with lingering notes of alcohol, making me wish I could literally drink her in. I nip at the base of her neck, catching some of the juniper mash with my tongue, earning me another shiver.

"I am literally covered in booze berries." She giggles, squirming in my arms. "Nothing about that is sexy."

"I beg to differ," I whisper, nibbling her earlobe. This time instead of a shiver, Rose coos, leaning into me. "Just means I have to use my tongue."

Rose lets out a long, low moan, her body relaxing into mine even more. I return to the base of her neck, nipping again, working my way up, as one hand slips into the tiny sleep shorts she's still wearing. The soft cotton gives easily, allowing me access to her—soft, smooth skin greeting me.

Enjoying the attention, Rose squirms again, and my other hand slips under her top, heading up toward her breast. My dick twitches, the curve of her ass cradling it nicely. She must feel it, because she wiggles her hips, encouraging me closer to her wetness but also giving my cock a taste of the attention he craves.

"Ohhhh," Rose moans, my fingers finding her nipple and clit at the same time.

Excitement rushes through me, loving her reactions. She's so wonderfully vocal, not afraid of sharing how she's feeling. In or out of bed. That's something I've come to admire over the last couple of days as we've gotten to know each other. But especially in moments like this. All her moans, murmurs, coos—each new sound sending a rush through me. Letting me know that I'm having the same effect on her as she is on me.

I continue my attentions, switching to the other side of her neck, licking and sucking at the berry residue, making sure to get every last drop, careful enough not to leave a mark. Her skin is fresh and light, reminding me of something I can't name. Whatever it is, it's the perfect mix with the berries, leaving me wanting more.

So, so much more.

I want to taste her. All of her. I want to know if other parts of her are going to make me as wild and animalistic as her kisses do. If the rest of her is just as irresistible as what I've experienced so far.

I'm willing to bet good money that it is.

And I can't wait.

I give her nipple one last squeeze and flick her clit once more before pulling away. Rose gasps, eyes flying open as I spin her around, mouth agape in surprise. The flush on her cheeks is adorable, as is the look of longing in her eyes. I can tell she didn't want me to stop, and her body is silently protesting my sudden actions.

Oh, just you wait, darlin'...

"I think it's time we got you out of these clothes," I whisper, giving her a wink. "They're in my way."

I don't wait for a reaction, tugging her shirt over her head, quickly followed by tugging her shorts down too. In a matter of seconds she's standing before me, gloriously naked, looking good enough to eat. No, devour.

"Holy fuck..."

Rose giggles nervously, the pink in her cheeks deepening. My cock surges at the sight, somehow becoming even harder than before. Something I wouldn't have thought possible. At least not until I saw the goddess before me like this.

"Like what you see?" Rose asks, in a voice that is both timid and teasing. Like she doesn't know if she should be bold or self-conscious. I need to assure it's the former, and never the latter.

"No," I answer, stern and gruff. I grab hold of her hips, yanking her into me. Our bodies collide, air rushing from me thanks to the impact. "I more than *like* it. You are fucking stunning. My only problem is I don't know what to taste first."

"Pierce—"

I stop her protestations with a kiss. Hot, hard, and with a thrust of my hips, leaving no secret that I'm hard and so fucking turned on. She whimpers, reaching down to palm my erection. Oh, fuuuuck, does that feel glorious. But not yet. I need to taste her first. Need to hear her screaming my name until she's nothing but a puddle from her pleasure.

Then my dick can come out to play.

"Tell me, baby, what do you want?"

"You..."

"You have me. But I need to know where you want me. Where you want my tongue."

I slide my hand slowly down her body, stopping first at her breast. I circle one nipple, then the other, giving each taut peak the same treatment.

"Here?" I ask, before moving south, tickling my way down her belly. When I get to the smooth skin leading to her pussy, I take another moment to tease. Rose inhales sharply, and I know I've found my answer. But I still want to hear the words. Lazily, I slide my finger over her clit, through her folds, and into her. She's so wet I slip in easily, my mouth watering in anticipation. "Or here?"

"Yes!"

"Say the words, baby. Where do you want my tongue?"

"There. Please. Don't make me beg."

"Begging isn't required," I say, drawing my finger out, then in, then out again, toying with her entrance. "All you have to do is say the word."

"My pussy. Please. Please play with my pussy."

Without another word, I drop to my knees. I inhale deeply, holding my breath for a moment, like an addict with a much-needed cigarette. Rose is just as much of a drug, one that goes straight to my head, driving me insane with need. My head is cloudy with lust, my raging hard dick straining against my pants, dying to be freed. But more than anything, I'm a man on a mission.

I will not be deterred.

Grabbing ahold of Rose's ass, I dive in, tongue immediately finding her clit. She lets out a yelp, hands flying to the back of my head for balance. She's going to need it, because I have one goal and one goal only—to make her see stars and for those knees to wobble in the process. Actually, maybe that's two goals. Either way, I'm not stopping until it happens.

I turn my focus on said goal, nibbling, licking, and sucking as I go. She tastes so incredibly sweet, like strawberries in the middle of summer, and I can't get enough. I need more. I need her to come. Which means I need better access, Keeping my mouth pressed to her core, I slowly walk her backward the few steps until she's up against the vanity. I don't want to stop, so I lift a leg, throwing it over my shoulder. With this newfound angle, I dial in on her clit, sucking hard.

"Oh, shit!" Rose screams. "Right there, yes...right, fucking, there!"

I follow her directions, flicking my tongue rapid fire against the bundle of nerves that is now calling the shots for my girl. Giving her ass a firm squeeze, I let one of her cheeks go, working my way around her leg and up the inside of her thigh. Rose is so lost in everything she's feeling, she barely notices, until I slip two fingers inside her, seeking out that spot I already know drives her crazy. I find it quickly, giving it a light tap, just as I did last night.

"Pierce!"

The pitch of her voice could shatter glass, the last part of my name dropping off as a keen takes over. But I don't let up. I keep going, her pussy clamping down on me like a bear trap. Her hips buck against my mouth, my tongue still trained on that sweet spot that I know pushes her over the edge. She doesn't fight it, letting her orgasm rip through her like a tidal wave, unintelligible sounds echoing off the bathroom walls.

When she's finally done a long moment later, she slumps against the vanity, still holding on to my hair for balance. I push to my feet, making sure I hold on to her, not only to ensure her knees don't give way, but because I don't want to lose contact with her. It's like our bodies are tethered together with an invisible string, a connection that only we know about.

"Pierce..." Rose says again, this time much softer, her voice breathy.

"We're just getting started."

Scooping her up, I take her back into the bedroom. This next part is going to require a soft backdrop, at least for one of us. Which one, well, I'll let Rose decide that.

"I want you inside me," she declares, kissing me hard as I deposit her on the bed.

"Great minds think alike."

I continue to kiss her, disrobing as fast as I can. It feels like it takes forever, each article of clothing getting stuck around each turn, but finally, I'm free. My dick springs to life, thankful to be free from the confines. Turning my attention back to Rose, her eyes glued to my cock, licking her lips, a whole new surge of lust rushes through me. The thought of her mouth on me is the stuff dreams are made of. But so is sinking deep into her, and that's what I intend to do.

"You got three choices, gorgeous," I growl, the beast inside me ready to take over. "On all fours, on your back, on top. Take your pick."

Heat flashes in Rose's eyes. I can tell she immediately knows her answer, but she pretends to think a moment. I'm about to start counting to three and then choosing for her, when she speaks.

"All fours."

Her answer surprises me, as does how quickly she gets into position. Little miss sunshine is dirtier than I thought. Wiggling her ass as she widens her knees, showing off that gloriously wet pussy, she looks over her shoulder at me, giving me a come and get it look.

Don't mind if I do.

I sheath myself in record time, grabbing her hips and

lining myself up. She wiggles again, the anticipation getting to both of us. So I don't waste any more time. I sink in—slow, deep, purposefully, enjoying the heat enveloping me. Oh fuck. If I thought her pussy was fantastic before, it's leveled up now. She's tight, wet, and feels like home. The moan she lets out as I push in only furthers the ecstasy that I'm feeling.

"You're so tight..." I mutter though gritted teeth, right as she exclaims, "Fuck, you feel good."

I hold still for a moment, enjoying this feeling. But I don't stay that way for long. I want more. We want more. So I draw back, then piston forward.

"Yes!"

Rose's scream is the key to the cage, freeing my internal beast. I let go, let him take over. I pound into her, hard, fast, and with abandon, focused on nothing but the extreme pleasure coursing through me. Rose meets me thrust for thrust, her own sounds of delight mixing with mine. This woman is so incredible, her energy infectious, pushing me toward that edge. I can feel the base of my spine starting to tingle, and I know I won't last much longer. There's no way with this hot, tight, feral goddess matching my movements.

Reaching around her, I yank her upward, continuing to thrust inside her. Same as earlier, one hand lands on her tits, squeezing her nipple, while the other heads straight to her clit. The swollen bud is slick with her wetness, making it easy to circle. Rose cries out, her body starting to buck and convulse.

She's close. I can tell. Having wrung multiple orgasms from her already in the last twenty-four hours, I know the signs. And they are all there. So I continue, not stopping until I feel her pussy squeeze my cock for all it's worth.

Rose keens, just as my own climax hits me, a freight train slamming into a bed of feathers on the track, sending me flying into a million pieces. I roar as it rushes through me, unable to hold back. I continue to fuck Rose hard, not wanting to lose this connection.

In a tangle of sweaty limbs, we tumble onto the bed, both of us out of breath. We're silent for a long moment, nothing but the sounds of our racing hearts filling our ears. There's so much I want to say, but words fail me. How is it possible to say anything after an experience like that?

"Well, you certainly succeeded in making me dirtier," Rose jokes, rolling over to rest her head on my chest. Her skin is warm, inviting, and I can't help but wrap my arm around her.

"That was the goal."

"I guess now it's really time to clean up."

"Do you like bubble baths?" I ask, an idea popping into my head.

"Huh?" She lifts her head to look at me, brows knit together.

"Do you like bubble baths?"

"Yes…"

"Interested in joining me in one?"

Her eyes light up like a small child who just realized Santa had visited, smile growing by the second. Nodding furiously, she giggles. "Absolutely. And I like *lots* of bubbles."

"Lots of bubbles it is then."

11

ROSE

"CATCH YOU ON THE FLIP-FLOP, Big Ben, and Merry Christmas! This's been Rubber Duck!" a voice crackles through the radio.

I hold back my giggle, which is no easy task. Pierce's best friend, Lou, who I was just introduced to via the radio call, is quite the character. Loud, out there, and clearly a ham, he's quite the opposite of Pierce's stoic, dry-humored introvert. Probably why they make a good pair. Opposites do attract, after all.

Pierce hangs the hand controller back up on the side of the receiver, rolling his eyes at his buddy's sign-off.

"Big Ben?"

"Yeah. When I first drew up plans for this place, Lou insisted we get the radio. Said that with cell reception being what it is, they needed a way to be able to get in touch with the people in town. He's been big into it since college, talking with people all over the world via that thing, so he taught Gramps how to use it, then offered to be their point of contact should they need anything and the phones be out. Anyway, he insisted we all needed call signs."

"That's so cute!"

"Cute is one word for it," Pierce scoffs. "He's been Rubber Duck from the start. In high school he drove this beat to shit, bright yellow VW bug. One year as a joke, another friend and I painted it to look like a rubber duck. Lou thought it was hilarious and kept it. So, when he needed a call sign in college, it was like he had one built in. He gave Gram the name Cheshire Cat, for obvious reasons, and Gramps was Moneypenny."

"Your grandfather's call name was the secretary in James Bond?"

"Yup. Because he used to tell us as kids that the reason he asked Gram out was because she looked just like Miss Moneypenny in the Bond films—'only prettier.' So, Lou thought it was funny to call him that."

"And you got Big Ben because you were in London?"

"Indeed. I guess it was better than being QE2."

I giggle again, loving seeing his sense of humor shining through. He comes and joins me on the couch, taking the side with the wayward spring, and I can't help but think about how different he is from when I first got here. Or, maybe he's not different. I suppose the man who slammed the door in my face is still in there, somewhere. But that's not who he really is. I've seen a completely different side of him come out. A side I really like.

And I don't mean that simply because he rocked my world last night, delivering mind-blowing orgasms and world-class snuggles. Four of those orgasms to be precise.

No, this goes beyond that. We've bonded. Formed an unexpected, unusual friendship. The kind that can only come by being forced together due to weather and unnavigable roads. If you'd told me two days ago that I would actually like Pierce and enjoy spending time with him, I would have laughed. There was no way. But the more we talk, share, and laugh, the more and more I want to continue to do those things with him.

And more.

Because Pierce might just be the best kisser I have ever met. Those damn things set my soul on fire, and I'm not sure that anyone is going to be able to kiss me that well after I leave here. My heart squeezes at that thought. Leaving. I do want to leave. I want to get home to my family. Not being with them right now hurts in a way I can't describe. On the flip side of that coin, though, I know it's going to hurt to leave Pierce. Not on the same level as missing my family on Christmas, but it will hurt. I can only hope we can maintain a friendship after this.

"You look lost in thought," Pierce says.

I shake my head and blink, snapping back to reality. I hadn't realized I'd slipped away, but the expectant look on his face tells me that I clearly missed some things he's said in the last few minutes.

"Sorry, drifted off a bit, I guess."

"Can I ask where to?"

"Where else? Hickory Hills." I giggle, hoping it will keep my tone light. All it does, though, is sound awkward and forced. The last thing I want is for Pierce to think that I'm not enjoying his company. Because I am. I just also wish I was with my family.

"It's hard for you not to be with them, huh?" he asks, understanding in his voice.

I nod. "Yeah. This is the first Christmas I've spent away from them. That probably sounds really lame, but we're a close group. Plus, it's Tizzy's first one with us, and I've been wondering if Cary was going to propose on Christmas morning as everyone opened gifts."

"I have a phone, you know. You can call them. Find out if Dizzy is now a carat heavier."

I bark out a laugh, both at his incorrect name for my soon-to-be sister-in-law and his way of referencing a ring. See, there's that dry humor. I love it.

"Tizzy. With a T." I make the timeout symbol with my hand to illustrate. "Although, she'd probably make you dizzy. I know she did Cary when they first met. She's a free spirit if there ever was one, and can kinda be all over the place at times. But, she has such a big heart and is so wonderful. They even each other out really well."

"You two must be like two peas in a pod then, with all that energy."

"Oh, she makes me look like a slug at the pace she moves," I joke.

Pierce's eyebrows fly upward in surprise. Like he can't believe that anyone would be more energetic than I am. He must not know very many people then, but I don't think I rank all that high.

"You act like I'm a chihuahua on speed," I continue, giving him a playful kick. "And I am nothing of the sort. I might be like a cute little Corgi puppy, but..." I trail off, getting lost in the tender look Pierce is giving me. It's making my insides do funny things, and I'm not sure if I like it or not.

Okay, fine. I like it. A lot.

"Come with me."

Pierce abruptly pushes up from the couch, taking my hand and yanking me off too. I stumble for a second, trying to catch my balance from the quick reshuffle, but manage to do so as we make it to the hallway. At first I'm confused, wondering what on earth he's doing. That is, until he leads me into his office. Now I'm even more confused.

"What's your brother's number?"

"Why?"

"We can call him." He points to his insane monitor setup, settling himself in the desk chair, like it should be the most obvious thing in the world. "Send him a text and tell him to be ready to accept a call from Adams Moneypenny Investments. It'll likely come over as the company name, rather than a number."

"Do you have some magic trick to making texts go through? Because I think I've managed like two since I've been here thanks to the reception."

"Wi-Fi?"

"You have Wi-Fi?"

My voice is incredulous which, paired with the stupefied look on Pierce's face, makes us quite the pair. He's looking at me like I'm crazy, but he told me there was no Internet when I got here, so unless he pulled that out of a hat without my knowing, I'm not the crazy one here.

"Have you not been connected to the network for the last three days?"

"Network? What network? You said there was no Internet."

"Yeah, because of the storm."

I shake my head in disbelief. That was not what he said. Such a man thing to do. "That is not what you said. You said there was no Internet. As in period. None. Not because of snow."

Pierce shrugs, like there wasn't much of a difference. "How'd you think we watched the movie? Or I do my work?"

I stop, mouth open, ready to argue, but I can't. I suppose that he could have owned the movie—that wouldn't have been too much of a stretch. Working, however...he had me there. I snap my mouth shut, suddenly feeling rather dumb. I can't believe it didn't occur to me that he could have meant there was no Internet in the moment, or to even ask after the fact. He and I didn't communicate all that well at first, so it shouldn't be surprising that we had a baby misunderstanding.

"Clearly, I was not thinking about any of that."

Reaching out, Pierce places his hands on my hips, tugging me into him. I step in between his open legs, this gesture of affection sending butterflies through my veins. It feels easy, natural, like we're any other couple, standing here talking. Slipping my arms around his neck, I lean into that feeling, letting it settle around me. Because it's wonderful. Even if it is only temporary.

Pierce tightens his grip, pulling me closer, until we're only a whisper apart and he can kiss me. It's soft, gentle, and matches that easy naturalness that I'm already relishing. When his tongue meets mine, those butterflies turn to puppies, every part of my body alert and pushing each other out of the way to try and be the next one to get attention.

I moan, ready to give in and mount him right here, but he pulls back. I miss him instantly—the feel of him, the heat of his body, all of it. I mask it though, not wanting him to think that I'm only in this for his dick.

Which, fuck, might be the best one I've ever encountered.

Focus, Rose...

"Give me your phone, and let me get you connected. Then we can text your brother."

I hand Pierce my phone, watching as his fingers fly over the screen, connecting me to the Wi-Fi. My phone comes alive with dings and trills from all the notifications I've missed over the last few days. The high-pitched racket makes me realize how nice it's been without all that. Maybe I need to take an unplugged weekend more often.

Fifteen minutes later, after Cary has responded to my text, the computer is dialing and Pierce is shuffling me into the spot he'd been sitting in. My heart is beating a million miles a minute, the rest of me so nervous and excited I don't know whether to laugh or cry. Which sounds ridiculous. This is my family. Considering not even an hour ago I was having a pity party that I couldn't see them on Christmas, this is the best thing that could ever happen.

"Hello?" Cary's voice says, the camera taking a moment to engage. A split second later, he appears on the screen, his handsome face and dark hair overwhelming me. Cue the waterworks. "Rosie! There you are!"

"Hi!" I exclaim, waving wildly. "Merry Christmas!"

"Merry Christmas."

"She there?" Tizzy asks. The picture wobbles and I bite back a laugh. It doesn't take a genius to know that she's wrestling the phone out of his hand. "Rose! OMG, girl, you okay?"

"I'm fine. No, more than fine. I'm great. I got to go sledding."

"Seriously? I'm officially jealous. I've never been. Tell me all about it!"

I launch into the story, starting with my snowman, moving on to the kayak, and finally arriving at the real sled that Pierce busted out. I tell her all about our many runs, and how much fun we had. I leave out the part about the panty-melting kisses though. At least for now. I'll tell her all about it once I'm back in Hickory Hills. But for now, with my brother there, not a chance. I also know my mother, father, and potentially my grandparents are also circling around like vultures, waiting for their turn. And I most certainly am not making the details of last night known to them. The idea that I responded to the command of "on all fours, on your back, or on top" with "all fours" is not information that Grandma needs to know.

Tizzy passes the phone to Mom, who gushes over how rested I look. My cheeks turn warm, and I look away, locking eyes with Pierce. He smirks back, like he can read my thoughts. Because again, it's all thanks to him.

"Is the nice gentleman who helped rescue you there? Can

I meet him?" my mother asks, her thick southern drawl slicing through the air.

Nice gentleman. If you only knew, Mama...

"He is..." Pierce's eyes go wide as I wave him in closer, panic fluttering in his pupils. I nod, trying to assure him that she won't bite him via an Internet call. Slowly, he comes into the frame, still looking nervous. "Mama, this is Pierce Adams. The, err, nice gentleman who helped rescue me."

Pierce scoffs under his breath, quickly trying to disguise it as a cough. Mama doesn't seem to notice though, her bright smile growing on her face.

"Oh, he's handsome, Rosie."

"Real person, Mama. He can hear you..."

"Hi Mrs. Adler. Nice to meet you!"

"Nice to meet you, Pierce. Thank you so much for hosting our Rosie. I'm sure it wasn't what you had planned this holiday, but knowing she's safe makes this Mama's heart so happy."

"My pleasure."

He coughs again, but this time it's different. I look at him closely, noticing the new shine in his eyes. Biting his lip, he nods awkwardly. If I didn't know better, I'd think he was—oh shit, he is. Pierce is fighting back tears.

My heart aches, realization hitting me. He might be a stoic grump, but there's a reason behind it. He doesn't have a family. During a time of year that does nothing but rub that in your face. And here he is, helping me connect with mine. I need to make this up to him. Show him just how much I appreciate what he did.

Turning back to my mother, I continue the conversation, steering it away from Pierce, which allows him to exit quietly. We continue on for a while, every member of my family taking a turn, showing off what Santa brought and sharing a story from the time I've missed with them. It does my soul good to do this. It's not the same as being there, but it's the next best thing.

When we finally hang up, I turn to find Pierce, but he's not in the room. I switch the monitors off, then tiptoe into the den, looking for him. He's sitting in front of the fire, holding a silver frame containing a photo of an older couple. I don't have to ask to know who it is.

"Thank you."

"Of course."

He looks up at me, his eyes still shiny and slightly red. My body wants to rush to him, to hold him and comfort him. That's not what Pierce needs though. That's not who he is. So, I offer up one of the few things I have at my disposal.

"Was there something Gram used to make every Christmas?"

He doesn't even have to think about the answer. "Meatballs."

I smile, loving how quickly he responded. As if the memory is still so alive for him that he half expects to find her in the kitchen right now making them. Actually, he probably does, and that's what stings the most.

Holding out my hands, I give him a wink. "Then I think it's time we made meatballs."

12

PIERCE

I SMILE and bite back a laugh, admiring the brunette beauty currently taking over my kitchen, one hand on her jutted-out hip, the other in the air, doing a math problem.

I could just eat her right up, Gram would have said. And she would have been right. Her pretty pink mouth pursed together and quirked to one side as she thinks, her brows tucked inward, is the kind of look that could bring any man to his knees. Heaven knows, she's already brought me to mine. Literally.

Sliding up behind her, I place a kiss right where her neck and shoulder meet, inhaling her sweet scent. How she still smells so intoxicating after three days with nothing but my unscented bar soap, I have no idea. But I'm not complaining.

Rose squirms, her backside rubbing against the semi I'm already sporting, a jolt rushing through me. "You made me lose count."

"Ooops."

Except I'm not sorry. Not sorry at all.

I peer over her, eyes scanning over the recipe card decorated with pale purple flowers, strategically placed in the card holder in the middle of the island. I've read it a million times and could probably recite it if needed, however, tonight it seems brand-new. The woman currently wiggling her hips against my dick probably has a lot to do with that.

"We don't have everything we need," Rose continues. "Or at least not *enough* of it, so I need to halve the recipe. And I get a little weird with fractions."

I bite back another laugh, not wanting her to think that I'm laughing at her. At least not in a mean way. She's just so damn cute.

I step back, giving her the space she needs to "get weird with fractions." I try to think about what we need, other than the ingredients Rose has already pulled out. Gram had this down to a science, and didn't even have to think about where she kept things. If we were back in their old house in town, then this probably wouldn't require as much thought on my part, but I'm still learning where she stored the non-everyday items. Like the purple ceramic mixing bowl with Cheshire Cat's tail painted on it that she used for just this occasion.

A few minutes—and a couple of wrong cabinets—later, I've found the bowl and pulled out the baking sheets. Sometimes Gram would use parchment paper when baking, but fuck if I know where that is, and no part of me feels like searching for it. So, I opt to spray the sheets down with the canola oil spray perched on top of the oven.

Rose coughs, wafting her hand in front of her face, trying to dissipate the cloud of aerosol.

"Easy there, killer. Don't want us coated in oil."

Sure about that...?

Rose winks, clearly reading my mind. Oh, this is dangerous. *She* is dangerous.

I inhale slowly, letting my lungs fill all the way, making sure I exhale just as slowly, reminding myself this is about a cherished memory. About continuing on Gram's tradition. Not about playing grab ass with my house guest.

Even if Gramps used to always swat Gram's backside when she was cooking.

"I've got everything mathed out properly…I think…so, what's first?" Rose asks.

"It's on the card."

Rose huffs. "I am aware, but this isn't just about reading the directions. It's about experiencing the process."

"Experiencing the process? You sound like one of those new age gurus."

"Pierce!"

Mouth in a scowl and hands on her hips, Rose glares at me. Fuck, even when she's grumpy she's cute. I grin back at her, trying my best to look just as cute, but I'm sure I'm not. What I am pretty sure I am accomplishing is looking as guilty as a five-year-old with his hand in the cookie jar.

"You're right, you're right," I acquiesce. "First things first, meat goes into the bowl."

Rose nods, following my directions. We continue on, me walking her step-by-step through the recipe, with her adding each ingredient, one by one, each with a little flourish. A wink, a giggle, a hip thrust. Each item gets something new, keeping me laughing.

Which, I have to admit, feels damn good. It's been a long time since I laughed like this or had this much fun in the kitchen. Especially while making meatballs.

Memories come flooding back, overwhelming me for a moment and leading me to do something that is so out of character yet feels so incredibly right.

Share.

"Some of the best conversations I've ever had were with Gram while rolling meatballs. We used to sit and talk for hours as she made dozens of these things. She made them for every potluck, every meeting she attended, really any occasion."

"What did you talk about?"

"Anything. Everything. I admitted to having my first crush while making meatballs. Gram of course already knew, but I felt like it was the biggest secret in the world."

"Awwwww. I don't know that I ever told my parents about my first crush. That just seems...horrifying?"

I chuckle. "Yeah, well, Gram had a way of making you want to spill your guts to her. Her own brand of magic, if you will."

"I think it's amazing that you have that. Something to help keep her with you."

"I feel her everywhere in this house. Gramps only in the garage or basement, which, truthfully, would be the way he wanted it. Man places."

"Man places..." Rose shakes her head. "The kind of thing only a man would say."

I shrug, not knowing how else to respond. She's not wrong, but that was Gramps to a T.

"What do you use to mix everything?" she asks, not skipping a beat.

"Your hands."

"Hands?"

"Yup. Best way to make sure it all combines properly," I tell her, reciting Gram's spiel. "So, get ready to manhandle that meat."

"Oh, I'll manhandle your meat..." she mutters under her breath.

Fuuuuuuuuuuuck....

It just got a thousand degrees hotter in here. The semi I had been sporting, well...there's nothing semi-hard about my dick now. It's full-on hard.

Rose blushes, realizing she said that out loud. I smirk

back at her, wanting her to know that I liked it. A lot. Because despite how this all started, I like Rose. A lot.

The kind of like that twists you up inside. That makes you want to be around them, no matter what they're doing. The same kind of like that I first admitted to while making meatballs with Gram. Only, this goes deeper than a crush. Rose is exactly the kind of woman I could see myself with. That in itself is a wild, borderline-unsettling thought. Because settling down has always been a someday thing. Something far away in the future.

Then again, that was before Rose Adler walked into my life.

Giving me a quick smile, Rose turns back to the bowl. I lean against the island, watching as she sucks in a deep breath, her chest rising as she inhales, my eyes glued to her. My insides go mushy, more emotions than I've let through in a while surfacing. Not all of them are sad though. In fact, most aren't. More than anything, they're warm, fuzzy, and are all about Rose.

"I'm going in!"

True to her word, with all her effervescent energy, Rose dives in, almost attacking the ground beef in the bowl. Squishing her hands through it, she scrunches her face, then lets out a giggle that bounces off the walls, settling in my chest. I watch, still unable to look away, as she continues to mix, indeed manhandling the meat.

"Go gentle," I say.

"You want me to be gentle with your meat? Not how I had you pegged," she quips, throwing a flirty look over her shoulder.

Oh, two can play this game.

I push up from where I'm leaning and turn to face her, extending my arm. Before Rose can react, my hand connects with her ass, the smack ringing into the air, same as her giggle had just done. Rose gasps, half turning to look at me. She glares and I return her look, one eyebrow quirked up, inviting her to retaliate. I know she can't though, since her hands are currently occupied.

What I get is the most Rose response there is. She sticks her tongue out at me.

And fuck, does it make my insides do somersaults.

"Gentle..." I repeat, this time in a softer, less playful tone.

Sliding up behind her, making sure her back is flush with my front, I wrap my arms around her. I take a moment to revel in the feel of her against me—her curves, her soft skin, her warmth. If there is a heaven, this might just be it. I run my hands along her arms, slowly, gently, not wanting to rush the moment. When my hands reach hers, I cover them, sinking them into the mixture. It's cold and gooey, a sharp contrast to my overheated skin, taking me a moment to get used to. Once I do though, I start to move, guiding Rose's hands in time with mine.

"See, gentle," I whisper into her ear. "Combining the ingredients is an act of love. It's not sharp, or harsh, but delicate. They should mingle together, each maintaining their own unique flavor, while bringing out the best in each other."

Rose relaxes into me, letting out a sigh. My cock twitches against her ass, earning me a wiggle. I tighten my arms around her, wanting to be as close as possible.

"You make it sound so..."

"So..."

"Euphoric."

"I dunno about that," I reply, placing a kiss on her neck. She shivers from my touch, so I do it again and again, moving my way up to her ear. I nip at her earlobe, then whisper, "But done right, it is an experience."

I no longer have any idea if I'm talking about cooking or something else. But it doesn't matter, because the breathy gasps and sighs from Rose let me know that she's right here with me. That our hands intertwined, covered in gooey goodness, is the start of something. The furthering of a connection. One that I don't want to break. Potentially ever.

Turning my focus back to her, I work my way down the other side of her neck. She lets out a low moan, her breathing picking up, body pushing into mine with every inhale. I'm so turned on, my rock-hard dick begging to be set free. My mind flashes with a series of dirty thoughts—all the things I could do to Rose right now. Sit her on this counter and feast on her glorious pussy. Bend her over and fuck her until we're both screaming. Splay her out on the table, pouring my latest batch of gin all over her body and licking her clean.

But none of that seems right.

No, what feels right is holding her close. Enjoying the moment. Staying caught in the spell she has me under, committing this to memory, so that I can remember for the rest of my days.

Because my time with her is limited. I don't know when I stopped counting down until the de Baers called, but now I'm starting to wonder if I can put it off. Or find a way to convince her to stay. She's a salve for my soul that I didn't realize I needed.

"Pierce," she whispers, arching her back, pressing her shoulders into my chest.

"Yeah, baby?" I return, still lost in our trance.

"I…I want…need…" she trails off, eyes fluttering shut as I nip at her skin.

"What? What do you need?"

Even in the hushed tone, I can hear the gravel in my voice, my own need shining through.

"You."

13

ROSE

Meatballs are forever ruined.

Never again am I going to be able to look at one and not think about this moment. The feel of Pierce's lips on my skin, nipping at my neck. The heat radiating off him. The hardness of his erection pressed against my ass, making me feel like the most wanted woman in the world. His arms wrapped around me, our hands intertwined as we lose ourselves in whatever this is.

My statement lingers in the air, swirling around us, tugging at our hearts. Or, well, mine anyway. Although the groan Pierce lets out leaves me pretty sure I'm not alone in that.

He presses a kiss right where my neck and shoulder meet —a spot I didn't know was so sensitive until Pierce. Now, just the idea of his lips there makes my body warm, which is exactly what is happening now. Heat spreads through me, my insides turning squirmy, making me want to hand over control to him. Something else I never thought I'd enjoy. But there's something about Pierce that makes me trust him.

Something that I know deep down inside. How, I'm not

sure. But I *know* it. He's not going to hurt me. Not unless pain was on my wish list. Which it is not. He seems to know that too, without even asking. When he looks at me with those deep, dark eyes, it's like he's seeing into my soul.

"Pierce…" I say on a long exhale, more of those neck kisses eating away at my resolve. Or should I say *lack* of resolve.

I spin around, my body rubbing against his as I move, his erection even more prominent as it slides across my body. I open my mouth to continue, but Pierce cuts me off with a kiss. It's hot, heavy, and totally controlling, yet slow and deep. His tongue finds mine as he pushes me against the island with his hips, and his hands land on the granite with a smack, caging me in. I moan into the kiss, the simple thought of being pinned in like this almost too much.

"Shhhh," he whispers, pulling back just enough to nibble on my bottom lip. "Now's not the time for talking."

His mouth is on mine again, this time so fast I barely have time to catch my breath. Fuck, can this man kiss. Knees wobbling, lady bits standing at attention, I can feel myself growing wetter by the second, all from his kiss. He hasn't even grabbed a boob yet and here I am, revved up and ready to go.

Placing my hands on his shirt, I move them up over his pecs, wanting to drawing him closer. Until I remember.

Raw meat.

We were making meatballs.

I gasp, trying to pull back, my mind suddenly whirring with worry. I can feel the look of panic on my face, my hands frozen on Pierce's chest, sure that I just ruined the mood. Because nothing says unsexy like raw meat.

Leaning back, Pierce gives me a smirk, a single chuckle tumbling over his lips. He kisses my forehead, then my nose, and finally chastely on the lips, each one leaving a trail of heat in its wake. It sends a shiver through me, my body clearly confused on how it's feeling. Hot, cold, who knows. Turned on—that's the answer.

Turned all the fucking way on.

"Stay," he commands, but not like one would a dog. His voice is hard, leaving no room for questioning or debate, yet still gentle. One little word, but it holds the promise of so much more.

He turns around, messes with something at the sink, and in the blink of an eye is back, wet paper towel in hand. Starting at my elbow, he wipes me down, slowly, surely, in the same way that some men wax their car, every millimeter getting the same amount of attention. When that hand is clean, he does the other, again, not missing a single spot. Then, he opens a can of wipes on the counter next to me. Where did those come from?

Their distinct citrus scent fills my nostrils, leaving no doubt what they are. Pierce starts in the same place as he did with the paper towel, moving at the same languid pace. My heart leaps as the cloth glides over my forearm, followed by the drag of his rough fingertips. I fight back another shiver, trying not to let myself be overcome by this. Leave it to Pierce to make disinfectant sexy.

"All clean," he says, winking, wiping himself off, and dropping the wipes.

He places a hand on either side of me, caging me in again, leaning in so our foreheads are touching. I can feel his breath against my lips, calling out to me. I want to kiss him so damn bad, but I don't dare move.

"Here's the thing, darlin'." His voice is deeper than normal, his southern accent thick, dripping with a soulful lust that I feel to my core. "I can think of a hundred and one ways to take you. All sorts of things that are going to put us so high on the naughty list, that we might earn us a permanent spot."

This time, I can't stop the shudder. It starts at the top of my head and runs the length of my body, straight to my tiptoes, taking all the air in my lungs with it. I swear on Father Christmas himself that it just got a million degrees hotter in here. I'd think there was something wrong with the oven if I didn't know we hadn't even turned it on yet.

Nope, this is all Pierce. Him and that mouth of his.

"But I was taught that you eat your dinner at the table."

Oh fuuuuuuck…

I'm frozen, my mind going blank, the rest of me zinging with anticipation. I've never wanted to be dinner so badly in my life. I know what this man can do with his tongue—not to mention his hands, hips, and dick—and well, Pierce can be my guest and feast however he wants.

Pierce isn't frozen though. With a single waggle of his brow, he takes my hand, guiding me over to the small alcove off the kitchen where the table sits. The massive picture window shows off the beautiful view of the mountainside, sunshine streaming in, illuminating the old oak table. I'm in a trance, my heart racing, each new move a mystery as I wait for Pierce to say or do more.

He doesn't though. At least not at first. He's silent and still, eyes glued to mine, his broad chest moving in time with his breath. The warmth of the sun surrounds us, cocooning us in its rays, only increasing the intensity of the moment.

When he does finally move, all bets are off. The animal inside him is unleashed, his soul-stealing eyes going even darker, melting the little that is left of my insides. His hands are on my hips so fast I barely register them there before he's tugging down my leggings. Kneeling down to peel them off each leg, Pierce growls.

"No panties…"

His two-word statement is simple. Nothing more than an observation. One that makes my knees wobble and the wetness between my legs increase. Pierce can tell too, since he huffs out a laugh, widening my stance.

"And here I thought you were a good girl, Rose," he continues. "But here you are, no panties and a soaking wet pussy? I might need to reevaluate my assumption."

"No...no..." I reply, my voice breathy. It's like his words are sucking all the oxygen out of the room, leaving me gasping just to respond. "I'm a good girl, I promise."

I look down at him, his sly grin greeting me, making my knees even more unsteady. Seriously, he keeps this up and I'm not going to be able to stand.

"Is that so?" he asks, leaning in and quickly swiping at my wetness with his tongue.

"Yes!" I scream, although I'm not sure if I'm answering his question or simply crying out from pleasure.

Pierce laughs at my response. He doesn't continue though, making the ache I'm feeling for his touch grow right along with his grin. I'm glad he finds this amusing, because I feel like I'm ready to pop. I've never been this turned on, and from here, it's anyone's guess how my body is going to react.

Running his hands up the outsides of my legs, he continues past my hips, rising from his knees. He doesn't stop at the hem of my shirt, taking it with him and pulling it over my head. The cool air hits my overheated skin, my nipples contracting from the change.

"No bra either, tsk tsk..." He shakes his head, mocking disappointment. The excitement that flashes in his eyes gives him away though. I know that excitement all too well, my own rushing through my veins like it's running the Kentucky Derby. "Question is now, what first?"

I shake my head, eyes going wide, unable to form the words to answer. At this point, I don't care where he touches me, just as long as he does. And soon. I'm a ticking time bomb, craving a release that I know only he can give me.

Running his hand over my breasts, he flicks my nipple, watching me as I react to the pleasure. It's so damn good, and I want him to do it again.

"Tell me, beautiful, how should I start this meal? Here?" he asks, taking that same nipple and rolling it in his fingers. I moan, pushing my chest forward, asking for more. He doesn't give it to me. Instead, he lets go and trails his hand south, stopping only when it reaches my core. "Or here?"

I moan again, this time louder. Just as I did with my chest, I move my hips, trying to make contact with his fingers, but Pierce isn't having it. He's on to me, and isn't going to give me the satisfaction of any more teasing.

"Use your words, Rose. Tell me where you want me."

"Please..."

It's all I can manage, my brain a jumble as the desire to be touched takes over. I'm a live wire, ready to spark, and all I need is the right contact. Contact that Pierce is dangling in front of me like a carrot.

"Words, Rose. Be the good girl I know you are and tell me."

As if those words alone aren't dirty and delicious, the deep gravelly tone he says them in takes them to the next level. The one that makes me putty in his hands.

"My pussy. Please..."

"Dessert first. Don't mind if I do."

Before I can exhale, Pierce lifts me up, depositing me on the table. He buries his face between my legs so fast, I barely notice the slight movement from the table, my attention all on him and the attention he's giving me. Because, holy fuck...

"Gahhhhh!" I scream.

Pierce's tongue hits my clit, and I'm done. Rapid-fire

flicks, fast as hummingbird wings, mix with lazy circles and nibbles. He's everywhere, all at once. Hitting me in all the right spots. My eyes slam shut, hands flying to the back of his head, wanting—no, *needing*—to keep him right there. I'm so close, hanging on by a thread, just waiting for it to snap.

Then Pierce slips a finger inside me. Followed almost immediately by a second.

A bomb goes off inside me. As soon as his fingers hit that special spot deep inside me, I'm done for. My climax slams into me, sending me into a million pieces as I buck wildly against Pierce's mouth. He holds steady, gripping onto my thighs for dear life, not letting up, his tongue still moving at the speed of light on my clit.

A long moment later, the aftershocks of my orgasm still pinging their way through me, Pierce kisses his way up my body. My wasted, Jell-O-like body. I'm too spent to move, basking in the glow of the sheer intensity of it.

That is, until Pierce reaches my mouth and kisses me.

I can taste myself on his lips, tangy and sweet, his tongue seeking out mine like a missile. A new wave of lust zaps me back to life, and now there's only one thing I crave.

Him. Inside me.

"Fuck me," I mutter into our kiss.

"Is that an exclamation or a request?"

"It's an order," I quip, my desire making me brazen.

"Only I give the orders around here, darlin'." He deepens the kiss, hand landing on my breast, squeezing hard. Oh shit, does that feel good.

"You told me to use my words. I am. I need you, inside me, fucking me. Now."

"Good girl."

He steps back, taking a second to rid himself of his clothes, his hard cock springing free. Naked Pierce is a thing of beauty, and I let my eyes roam over him, soaking in the sight. Committing it to memory. Because fuck if I'm not going to think of him like this every time I need a little me time. This view is going to fuel more fantasies than I can count.

Producing a condom from what seems like thin air, he has himself dressed and ready just as quickly, stepping back to me. He kisses me again, this time slower, deeper, like he's passing on a message. One I receive loud and clear, even if I don't have words to put to it. We both know what we mean, that we're on the same page here. So I lean forward and line him up with my entrance, waiting for that glorious first thrust.

And I am not disappointed.

Pierce pistons into me hard and fast, filling me so completely it steals all my thoughts. Nothing exists right now except the feel of him. And it's more than glorious. It's magnificent. It's everything I need, more than I could want, and all that lies in between. He pulls back slowly, taking his time to hit that spot that he seems to have no problem locating. Focusing there for a moment, letting the head of his cock tease me, Pierce groans.

Then, all bets are off.

As if someone shot the starting gun of a race, Pierce finds his rhythm. It's fast, hard, and wild. Animalistic. He's a man possessed, unable to hold back. Which only lights the same fire in me. I wrap my arms around his neck, pulling him closer, trying to meet him thrust for thrust. We're a tangle of movements, grunts, groans, and who knows what else as we let ourselves go. The rest of the world is gone, and all that is left is the sunshine streaming in, hitting our bodies as we come together in a way that only we can.

Another orgasm brews within me, this one already feeling stronger than the last. Which shouldn't be possible, since the last one nearly wrecked me. Still, based on the rapid pace the telltale tingle is growing, I know I have no choice but to give in. To let myself go and let it take me where it's going to. My only requirement is that Pierce do it with me.

"I'm so close," I whisper.

"Good," he groans, somehow picking up the pace. "Be a good girl and come on my cock. Make me come with that pussy of yours."

His thumb finds my clit in an instant, his command still lingering in my ears. All of it combined is just what I need, the release that was hovering just below the surface rushing through me like a tornado and taking over. Every synapse fires at once, but my body goes rigid, fireworks blinding me, and the most intense, insanely incredible feeling I have experienced takes over. This is more than an orgasm; this is sheer ecstasy.

Forget meatballs. All future orgasms are ruined too—unable to live up to what Pierce does to me.

It's just that good.

Pierce lets out a roar, a deep, all-consuming sound that rumbles through me, reaching down into my soul. I feel his body spasm as he comes, his arms tightening around me, pulling me flush with him. He holds me like this for a solid minute, our hearts and heavy breaths intertwining.

Pulling away, I lean back, resting my weight on my hands. My heart is so full, my body satiated. This is not at all how I saw myself spending Christmas day, but now I can't think of anything better.

"Merry Christmas," I giggle.

Pierce groans, rolling his eyes. "Merry Christmas. And here I was thinking this day was gonna suck."

"That anything but sucked."

"Oh, I know, beautiful."

He winks, kisses me softly, and thrusts up into me again. I laugh, kissing him harder, wiggling my hips against him.

Only problem, the table wiggles with me. Pierce thrusts again and that's all it takes.

Crash.

The two of us collapse, right along with the table, landing on it with a hard, loud thud. Pain thrums through me, a sharp juxtaposition to the pleasure I'd just been feeling.

"Fuck."

I look at Pierce, his face twisted in a mix of pain and anger. It's then it hits me—this would have been his grandparents' table. Oh shit.

"I'm so sorry!" I cry, guilt taking over. "This was—"

"Yeah," he cuts me off. Rolling off me, he separates our bodies, with me groaning, not wanting him to go. "Gramps built it for Gram when they were first married."

"Pierce, I'm so sorry, I—"

"No. I put you on the table. This is on me."

His words aren't reassuring the way they're supposed to be. My heart breaks knowing that I am partly responsible for this. Pierce reaches forward and grabs one of the legs, examining it. It looks solid and steady, and up until a moment ago, I never would have believed anything else. Flipping it to look at the bottom of it, Pierce scowls. But something catches my eye.

"What's that?" I ask.

"A table leg."

"No. Inside it." I point to the top of the leg and the little bit of yellow sticking out. "It looks like paper…"

Taking a closer look, Pierce manages to grab ahold of a corner and pulls out a rolled-up piece of yellow paper. Unfurling it, his eyes scan the page, lips turning upward into a smile. Then he laughs.

A deep, happy laugh. One that sets my soul on fire.

"If you're reading this, the third time with wood glue was not the charm," Pierce reads out loud. "Maybe try listening to your wife and using better screws. Just never stop screwing her against the table. You still got it, old man."

He looks at me as he passes the note, tears in his eyes. My heart squeezing, I read it over again, noting that it was dated two summers ago.

"Gramps?"

"Told you he was a character. And that their love for each other was something else."

I nod, loving the way he talks about them. "I still feel bad we broke it. But at least we carried on tradition?"

Pierce guffaws, a happy tear escaping. "That we did. Meatballs and a broken table. Hell of a tradition." Turning to me, he smiles, that look returning to his eyes. "How about we take tradition to the shower and get cleaned up."

"Yes, please."

14

PIERCE

BANG! Bang! Bang!

The thunderously loud noise raises me from my sleep. I don't remember drifting off. The last thing I knew, Rose and I were curled around each other, a tangle of limbs, our bodies doing all the talking. Considering I'm still wrapped around her, both of us still naked, it stands to reason that we never made it any further than that.

Bang!

Alright...alright...

I unfurl myself from Rose, careful not to wake her. She looks like an angel, her soft brown hair splayed out on the pillow, her perfect breasts rising and falling gently with her even breaths, a serene smile on her face. Fuck, is she beautiful. Inside and out. Because it was going to take a special soul to un-grumpy my ass this weekend. And that's exactly what she did.

Throwing on the first pair of pants and sweater I can find, I amble toward the door, barely glancing at the mess we left in the kitchen. We finished up the meatballs—but only barely—and ate them in bed as we watched the original

Miracle on 34th Street. We did manage to keep our hands off each other during the movie—for the most part—since Rose insisted that we couldn't sully an innocent classic like that. She made a good point, but I told her that once the credits rolled, all bets were off, and there wouldn't be anything innocent for the rest of the night.

And there wasn't.

The banging starts up again, so I pick up my pace to the door. If it woke me, it could wake Rose, and that's the last thing I want. I want her still in bed, snoozing away, so I can return to her, rewrapping myself around her and waking her with my mouth whenever I'm done with whatever barbarian thinks it's okay to bang on doors at the butt crack of dawn on the day after Christmas.

I yank open the door, ready to let whoever is standing there have it, when I see Winston de Baer. I freeze, blinking hard, taken aback. He was the last person I was expecting to see here.

"Winston."

"Morning, Pierce!" he replies, way too chipper for the early hour. The sun is barely up, only the earliest pieces of sunlight starting to peek through the trees. "Got that spare you needed. I assume it's for the lime-green Jeep out by the gate?"

It takes a moment for it all to fully register. Winston de Baer is standing on my doorstep. Which can only mean one thing.

"How'd you get here? I thought the bridge wasn't supposed to be open yet?"

Winston shrugs. "That was the original thought, but it wasn't that bad. Only a portion of the roof collapsed. You know that one corner that was starting to sag? Well, that's what came down. Once the snow melted a little, it didn't take more than a couple of shovels full to remove the debris and make it passable. No biggie."

No biggie.

Except, it was. Is. It's very much a "biggie."

I've had a stranger in my house for four days because we thought the bridge was impassable. That it needed a lot more than some shoveling. Did they turn out to be an amazing few days with an incredible woman? Yes. But neither of us had any way of knowing that.

Moreover, it meant that Rose missed Christmas with her family for nothing. That she was stuck here with me when she could have had all that magic with them.

My heart squeezes, hating that thought. I know firsthand the pain that comes with missing your loved ones over this damn holiday. Hell, it's something Rose and I bonded over. When we didn't need to, because she could have been with hers. Fuck.

"So, yeah, the Jeep?" Winston asks, pulling me back.

"Err, yeah."

"Great! I'll get to changing it then. Since the gal gave me the size tire over the phone, I was able to just bring it up with me. Once I get it on, she'll be good to go. No need to stop by the shop."

She'll be good to go...

His words ring in my ears, a bell of realization resounding, making my stomach drop. Rose will be good to go. As in leave. My gut knots up, the thought of her leaving weighing me down. Even more so than the guilt of her missing Christmas with her family when she didn't have to. Because I like having her here. A lot. And I don't want her to leave.

I thought we had more time. At least another full day. Time to spend together, watching movies, tasting the gin, maybe even trying to cook together again. More time getting to listen to her laugh and her energetic stories about the farm back in Georgia. All of her brightness filling in the cracks of the shell that was left of me, helping me to feel whole again when I thought I couldn't.

"Sounds good," I choke out. I nod, trying my best not to come off rude.

"Great! Send you a text when it's all done."

I nod again, starting to close the door, then stop. "Hey, Winston," I call out. He spins around, lifting his chin to ask what's up. "Do me a favor? Put it on my tab and I'll reconcile it when I'm in for my oil change next week."

"Works for me!" He gives me a thumbs-up and starts back down the drive.

Letting out a sigh, I gently close the heavy wooden door, trying my best not to let my emotions get to me. We always knew this was temporary. That there was an expiration date. Nothing more than a holiday fling while we were killing time snowed in.

Except my heart isn't having it.

Somewhere along the way, he got himself involved. Sneakily working behind the scenes, planting little seeds of attachment while I wasn't paying attention. Letting it look like my dick was the one in charge, when it was really my heart opening up for the first time in what feels like forever, carving out a Rose-shaped space. Stupid fucking organ.

None of that matters though, because she's leaving. She doesn't belong here. She belongs back in her little town, with her family, that farm, and her brewing company. Not with a semi-recluse of a stockbroker who secretly distills gin in his basement. She deserves better.

"Who was that?"

I look up, Rose's sweet, dreamy voice swirling around inside me, lighting me up. Dressed in nothing but one of my shirts that sexily hits her midthigh, she rubs the sleep out of her eyes as she walks toward me.

"Winston de Baer," I answer, my voice catching.

Shit, I can't let her see that. She can't know that with five simple words, Winston shredded my insides and turned my world upside down. That I'm suddenly a mix of mushy emotions inside, even more so than before. I know I can hide this. I've done it for the last year. If I can do it over Gram and Gramps, I can with Rose too. No biggie, to use Winston's phrase.

Rose shakes her head, Winston's name clearly not meaning anything to her.

"The de Baers own Gold's Gas and Garage. You talked to Winston the other evening during the storm. He brought a tire up for you, and he's changing it now."

"Oh! But I thought..."

"Yeah, apparently the damage wasn't as bad as originally thought, so they were able to clear it quickly. He's, errrr, working on it now, so it shouldn't take long. He said he'd text when he was done."

"Oh."

That's all she says. Oh. But that one sound sums it up. All my feelings, everything that I wish I could say but can't, right there. Oh.

The look on her face is unreadable. I can't tell if she's just as cut up as I am, trying to figure out the perfect response. If she wants to stay here as much as I want her to. Or if she's trying to figure out the most polite way to dash past me and run back to Hickory Hills as fast as that lime-green Jeep will take her.

We stand in silence for a long moment, neither of us saying anything. Neither of us wanting to be the one to make the first move. The unexpected happened over these last few days, and it was magical, and now that magic has been broken. Spoiled. We have to head back to reality. And let's face it, reality bites.

"I guess I should pack then," she finally says, hands toying with the hem of my shirt, fingertips grazing her thighs. My mouth waters, knowing what's under there, my whole body wanting to pick her up, throw her over my shoulder, and take her straight back to bed. But I don't. "Then I can get out of your hair. I've been in your way long enough."

"You haven't been in my way," I correct her, taking two large steps and closing the gap between us. "It's been quite nice having you here."

It's been quite nice having you here? Just when the fuck did I become an eighty-five-year-old woman? Internally, I'm kicking myself, but my mouth doesn't seem to follow along, not doing anything more than smiling. Like an idiot. Because that's what I am right about now. An idiot.

"It was nice of you to let me stay, and to humor me with the sledding and movies and meatballs and…" she goes from rambling to trailing off, her eyes darting to the side, like she's unable to look at me. "Anyway, it was all so very nice."

Nice. Nice. Because this has all been nice. Good to know that neither of us can think of a better word. A word that we've now said so many times, it's lost all fucking meaning.

I need to say something. Do something. Tell her that I'd like her to stay. Or that I'd like to see her again. Or at least keep in touch. Keep in touch? Great, now this sounds like a high school yearbook. Maybe I should throw in a "don't ever change" just to round out the cliché.

"Rose—"

A knock at the door cuts me off. For the love of all things, who the hell could it be now? I huff, turning back around, even more annoyed than I was being woken up early. I swear, this door has seen more action in the last week than it has the rest of its life combined. I yank it open, finding Winston standing there again.

"Hey man, sorry, you got a lug wrench by chance?"

"You're delivering my tire but don't have a lug wrench?" Rose asks from behind me, her voice incredulous. I can't blame her. I was about to ask the same thing; she just beat me to it.

"Oh, hi Miss, I err…" Winston leans over to address Rose, but then stops, a blush reddening his cheeks. Based on that reaction I'm going to guess he just realized she's not only not wearing pants, but is in my shirt. Rose, on the other hand, doesn't seem to care, her hip cocked out, one hand resting on it, and an expectant look on her face like he has five seconds to answer or she's going to whoop him. "I'm gonna blame the new girl. Just don't let Hudson hear me say that."

"Secret's safe with me. There should be one in the garage. Follow me." I nod toward the garage, stepping outside to take him that way. I pause with the door halfway closed, sticking my head back inside. "Be right back."

Rose nods, her awkward smile still in place. Shit. I better figure out what to say, and quick.

Five minutes later, Winston is back on his way and I'm headed into the house, no wiser on what I'm going to say to Rose. My head is a jumbled mess, torn between playing it cool and being that guy who wildly professes his love after the first date. Neither seem like the right move, but I'm still at a loss for what the right one is.

Heading toward the bedroom, I pause in front of Gram and Gramps's wedding photo. The two of them are smiling bright, their love and excitement shining through the black-and-white photo. Of all the moments I've wished they were still here so I could ask them for advice, this one might just top the list. Because they would know what to do. Each one would have their own sage advice on what to say and how to approach this. I'm on my own though, so here goes nothing.

I step back, pivoting to turn into the bedroom, when Rose

barrels out, tugging her suitcase behind her. She jumps when she sees me, hand flying to her heart.

"Oh, I didn't hear you come back in!"

"Sneaking out like a thief in the night? Do I need to count the silver?" I joke.

"There's silver? Damn it, I missed that," she jokes back. I laugh, thankful that there is still this ease between us. "Just don't go looking for those candlesticks anytime soon."

She gives me an exaggerated wink, and I let out a guffaw. "One less weapon for Colonel Mustard to choose from, I guess."

Rose laughs, a true genuine smile breaking free. It makes my insides turn to goo while also making my stomach ache. Because somehow I know that's going to be the last one of those I see.

"You're not at all who I thought you were when you first opened that door, Pierce. I misjudged you, so, I probably owe you an apology."

"Eh, I didn't make it easy, so...call it even?"

"More than." She smiles again, and my stomach starts to turn. "Thank you for letting me stay."

"You don't have to rush out. I could make you breakfast."

"Thanks, but I really should get on the road. Hickory Hills is still a good five hours from here, at least. And who knows with holiday traffic. So..."

"Right, yeah. You're right. Your family is probably dying to see you."

She nods, sucking her lips into her mouth, her eyes darting away from mine again. And we've gone awkward. Great.

"Thank you again for letting me stay."

"You're welcome any time," I tell her, my voice wistful. "If you're ever in the area..."

"Yeah! Of course. And if you're ever in rural south Georgia, or oh! Are you entering the Georgia Spirits Challenge?"

"The what?"

"The Georgia Spirits Challenge. It's this big competition in Atlanta where local brewers, distillers, etcetera enter their craft cocktails, home brews, and all that. Winner gets a bunch of money and their drink featured on bar menus all over the city. Brandt Rawlins, who is one of my bosses at Southern Brothers, has something he's entering next year, so we'll all be there supporting him."

I shake my head. "Don't know what I'd enter. The gin doesn't even have a name."

"Oh. Well, if you think of one and enter, I'll be there."

I nod, not knowing what else to do. Maybe professing my love would have been the better option. There's still time...right?

I open my mouth to start, but Rose speaks instead.

"Anyway, I should go. He's probably done with the tire by now. Thank you again. There's no one else I'd rather be all snowed in with."

Rose puts her hand on my arm, pushing to her tiptoes, and kisses me on the cheek. Her lips are soft, tender, and warm, leaving her mark. I can still feel them lingering there even as she pulls away, and I hope that I never forget this feeling.

"Bye, Pierce."

"Bye."

And then, she's gone.

15

PIERCE

"HOLD ON, so let me get this straight," Lou says, pointing his beer bottle toward me.

We're sitting in The Woodsman, a loud crowd surrounding us, forcing us to talk louder than we normally would. When Lou called and asked if I was up for grabbing a beer, I didn't hesitate to say yes, thinking that getting out of the house would be a good idea. I needed to get away from those walls in hopes to clear my head. Because now on top of seeing Gram and Gramps everywhere, I see Rose. Which is not boding well for my future.

"Beautiful girl knocks on your door in the middle of a snowstorm, you slam the door in her face like the asshole you are, but she's not having it so she knocks again and wears you down. You spend four days snowed in with this pretty little thing, and in that time manage to go sledding, watch old movies, make Gram's meatballs, and you let her in on the gin secret?"

And have the best damn sex of my life...

I keep that last part a secret though. Lou doesn't need to know that part. Which, in itself, says something about how

I'm feeling. No, not something. Everything. I've always told Lou about my hookups. Not in detail, but a generic, "yeah, I fucked her" kind of thing. With Rose though, it's different. What went on between us was different. She was different.

And the day and a half since she left have been absolutely fucking miserable.

"Pretty much," I answer, taking a sip of gin and tonic. It's good, but not near as good as it would be with what's in my basement. Or if it were a certain brunette sitting next to me instead of a tall, wiry electrician.

"Damn, man. You lucky SOB."

I nod. Don't I know it. Except, I blew it.

"So, when do you see her again?" he asks.

"Don't. She left. Went back to Georgia."

"But you got her number, right?"

"Nope."

Lou looks at me, eyes wide, mouth agape in disbelief. I can see the wheels turning in his head, trying to process my answer and come up with a reply. Taking a long gulp of my drink, I prepare myself for whatever crazy thing is about to come out of Lou's mouth. Only, there was no preparing for what he does next.

In a single, swift move, Lou reaches behind me and slaps me upside the head.

"Ow. What the fuck was that for?"

"Pierce, I've been your best friend since we were kids. I've watched you do a lot of stupid shit. Hell, half the time I was doing that stupid shit with you. But this, by far, is the stupidest. No, it's beyond that. It's crazy."

"Don't hold back, would ya?"

The words are dripping with sarcasm, but I know he's right. So much so, it's like a dagger to my already aching heart. Rose was...perfect. It's a big heavy word, but there isn't another one. She was everything that I would ever want in another person. Friend, lover, partner. Sure, it was only four days, but she understood me in a way no one else has. She knew what I needed and was a salve to a wound I never thought would heal.

Too bad I could never live up to being remotely what she needs in return.

"I am holding back," Lou continues. "You have no idea how bad I want to shake you right now, hoping that would knock some sense into you. A sassy, perky, smart brunette who loves old movies, cooking, and alcohol production—literally your dream girl—is dropped in your lap, and you not only don't realize that you love her but you didn't get her number? There are no words for that level of dumbassery."

Love? Who the fuck said anything about love?

I whip around to face my buddy, ready to refute this statement. Only, I can't. Instead, I sit there, mouth wide open, the realization hitting me. I fell for Rose Adler. Hard.

"And this is the part where you realize I'm right and start to kick yourself..."

I glare at him, turning back around. "Yeah, yeah..."

"So, whatcha gonna do about it?"

"Nothing. You might be right about my feelings, but that means nothing. Pretty sure she doesn't feel the same way. She wasted no time in packing her things and going when Winston knocked on the door."

"Unless she's just as afraid of her feelings as you are."

"Who died and made you Dr. Phil?"

Lou shrugs. "Sometimes you just know things."

"How about you just know things about your own personal life instead? And leave me to wallow in my own dumbassery, as you put it."

"Okay, okay. But, one last thing. What would Gramps tell you to do?"

Gramps.

Part of me wants to reach over and smack Lou for bringing him into this. But a bigger part of me can hear Gramps's voice, telling me what I already know.

"When it comes to the right woman, there's no such thing as making a fool of yourself. Fight for her, fight with her, but most importantly, don't give up the fight."

Damn it.

"That Silver Lining Sour is pretty good, huh?" the bartender asks Lou, cutting into my thoughts. "Southern Brothers really upped their game with that one."

"What?"

"Silver Lining Sour. It's the newest one from Southern Brothers Brewing. It's really popular."

Southern Brothers Brewing. That is the brewing company Rose works for. It is like someone has rung a gong, the reverberations rippling through me like a pebble tossed in a still pond. She might not have left her number, but she shared plenty with me about her life back in Hickory Hills. Including where she works. And where her brother works. And…

"Lou, that's it."

"What's it? Beer? Beer solves a lot, dude, but I don't think it's the cure for this."

"It just might be. Well, maybe not beer, but gin."

"Oh, this is gonna be good."

Yes, yes it is. As long as I don't fuck this up too.

16

ROSE

"WANNA TELL me why you look like someone burned your cocoa beans?" Tizzy asks, nudging my shoulder with hers.

The gesture knocks me out of my headspace, her question taking a moment to register. I blink, hard, trying to right myself. There's no use in pretending I was paying attention. I was miles away, both my brain and heart still in a mountain cabin just outside Mistletoe Creek, Tennessee.

Continuing to stall, I look around the bar, letting out a happy sigh at the turnout. When Milo and Brandt called me the day after Christmas, just as I was hitting the highway, to tell me they wanted to throw a last-minute New Year's Eve party at Pour Decisions—the Southern Brothers taproom here in Hickory Hills—I was a little skeptical that we could pull it off on such short notice. But I should know better than to underestimate those two. And Milo's younger sister, Willa, a former Miss Georgia, who pulled together a meet and greet with local boy and mega country star Dustin Wild overnight last year. A New Year's Eve party in five days must have been a cakewalk.

I'd jumped on the party idea though, welcoming it as a

distraction from the clumsy exit I'd just made moments before. I have no idea what I was thinking. Clearly, I wasn't thinking at all. Panicking was more like it.

My insides twist, Pierce's voice still echoing inside my mind as he tells me that the bridge is clear and that my tire is being changed. I wanted to run out that door and tell the mechanic to stop, that it was no longer as important as I'd thought. That I was right where I wanted to be. Instead, my good Southern manners came out and I offered Pierce an out by saying I should pack. An out that he took.

It's been quite nice having you here...

Now there's a Southern brush-off if I ever heard one.

So much for thinking we had more time. And so much for thinking that there was something building between us. That all those things we shared, along with the epic sex, were anything more than two people passing the time.

"I'm fine," I lie, looking at the bubbly strawberry blonde to my left. Her unruly waves flow over her bare shoulders, hiding the spaghetti straps of her dress, as she arches her brow to tell me that she doesn't believe me. "Really."

"Liar."

"I'm just tired. Been a weird, wild week, you know?"

"You mean because you accidentally spent Christmas holed up in a mountain cabin with a sex god? Only to return home and plan a party?" Tizzy giggles.

"Yes, that."

"Why don't you call him?"

"I didn't get his number. I was too busy..." I trail off, unsure about what word I'm looking for. "Tiz, I know this sounds crazy, but...I kinda fell for him. Yes, I know it was just a few days and we were all stuck in this bubble being snowed in, but...there was a connection. He made me feel things I never have. And I don't just mean because we had epic sex. I mean, like, I could see myself spending my days, nights, weekends, holidays, everything with him."

"I don't think it sounds crazy. I do think that if you really feel that way, you should drive your ass back to that small town of his, knock on his door, and tell him that."

I scoff. "And say what? Hi, thanks for taking my ass in off the street, putting up with me, and fucking me senseless to help distract both of us from the fact it's Christmas. As a form of repayment I'm here to profess my love and just overall look like the nerd asking the jock to prom."

"Not what I would go with. But, Rose...I've been where you are. So, trust me when I say I get it. Because I really, really do. And it's weird when you suddenly find the person you want to argue with about what's for dinner every night and you don't have his phone number. But there's nothing wrong with taking matters into your own hands either."

I sigh. I want her to be right. I know it all worked out with her and Cary, but I am not Tizzy Mitchell. Rose Adler is not impulsive or free-spirited like that. Despite how much I wish I was.

"When that knock on the door woke us up, I was in the middle of this fairy tale-like dream. I was wearing a yellow dress, similar to Belle's. It didn't have as many ruffles in the skirt, and there was more shimmer to it, but it had cap sleeves like the Emma Watson version. I walked down this massive staircase and Pierce was waiting at the bottom and he escorted me into this ballroom and I suddenly knew how to waltz because we danced and he held me close and..." I sigh. "When I woke up I was smiling like an idiot. And then I found out Blanche was being fixed, and the realization hit me that I'm not Belle, and he's not the Beast, and despite how it all started out, this one wasn't getting a fairy-tale ending."

Tizzy opens her mouth to respond, but is cut off by my brother appearing at her side.

"Rosie, mind if I steal this beauty for a moment?" Cary asks.

"Go for it. I didn't mean to monopolize her. Besides, I should check to make sure that everything is going okay. I'll catch you guys later."

I step around them, not waiting for a response, making my way to the storeroom. I'm not two steps into the large, cool area when I hear a voice cry out.

"Yes! Right there, fuck!"

I freeze. It takes another full second for me to fully register that voice—Willa Hayes. Oh shit. I slowly back away, completely cognizant that I just stumbled onto something I shouldn't have—and wanting nothing to do with it. It also occurs to me that now might be a good time to find Milo and keep him far, far away from here, allowing Willa her fun. She and I have never been super close but have always gotten along, and well, just because I can't be as happy as she sounds right now, doesn't mean she shouldn't be.

"Rose!" Brandt calls as soon as I shut the door to the storeroom. "Milo back there by chance?"

"Nope," I laugh. "I was just about to go find him though."

"If you find him, let him know our special guest is here."

Special guest? What special guest? I wasn't in charge of the guest list, but at the same time, I feel like that is a piece of information that would have been shared. Unless I missed it. Which, given where my thoughts have been all week, is entirely possible. My face must betray my thoughts, because Brandt laughs.

"Follow me, and I'll introduce you," Brandt says, nodding in the direction of the bar.

We weave our way through the crowd, dodging all the town's characters, trying our best not to get caught up in more than a quick hello with each one. It still takes us fifteen minutes, since both Hattie Burch and Gail Chamberlain—co-captains of our small town's rumor mill—stop us, offering up their opinion on improving the event for next year. Because, of course.

When we finally squeeze past the last cluster of guests, making our way to the small alcove in the far corner of the bar, we find Milo facing us, talking to a tall, muscular, dark-haired man who is turned toward him. This must be the "special guest." Whose backside, I must say, is fabulous.

OMG, focus, Rose...not the time...

"Hey Rose!" Milo greets. "Glad Brandt found you. I'd like..."

Milo's words fade into the noise of the party as the special guest turns around, and my heart stops. My stomach flips and my knees wobble just as my heart kicks back into high gear, a small, audible gasp escaping.

Pierce Adams is here.

"Rose."

His voice is deep, gravelly, and delicious, waking up all sorts of things inside me. Fuck, how does he do that?

"Pierce."

It takes everything I have to say his name, and still it comes out as a squeak. My heart is racing too fast for me to think. The only thing I can focus on is it clamoring against my chest. Because Pierce is here.

"We'll give you two some space," Milo says with a wink.

He and Brandt are gone before I remember to tell him to avoid the storeroom, but I can't worry about that now. Willa is on her own. Because the sexiest man I have ever met in my life is standing before me, a crooked grin on his face, looking like he could eat me for dinner.

And I would gladly let him.

"Hi beautiful," Pierce says.

Beautiful. He's still greeting me with that. My insides melt, and I grasp at something, anything, to respond with.

"Hi."

It's lame, but it's all I have.

"How's your family? Everyone happy you're home?"

"Y-yeah. They're...good. I...errr...just...Pierce..." I stumble. I take a moment, sucking in a breath that makes my lungs hurt, trying to find my words. "You're here. In Hickory Hills. H-how? Why?"

"You."

"Me?"

The answer doesn't make sense. He's here for me?

"Yes, you." He closes the gap between us with a few long steps, my stomach doing more somersaults. "I shouldn't have let you leave. At least not the way I did. I missed you the second you walked out that door, and after a few days of being miserable, I knew I had to come find you. Come tell you what you mean to me."

"Pierce, I—"

"Rose," he cuts me off, stepping into me more and cupping my jaw with his hand. His skin is warm against mine, and I lean into it. "You took me by surprise. There is no denying that. But you were exactly the magic I needed. Your laugh, your huge heart, and your ability to see the best in everything are...well, like nothing I've ever seen. Something I never knew that I required, until now. I don't want to go another day without you in my life."

"Me either."

"I've fallen for you, Rose. Call it Christmas magic, or whatever you like, but you stole my heart. And I don't want it back. All I want is you."

Tears prick at the corners of my eyes, the lump in my throat catching all the words I want to say, not letting any of them pass. All I can do is nod, my heart exploding with emotion.

"Please say something."

"Same, Pierce, same," I manage, tears escaping with my words. "I shouldn't have just left, but…I was…I don't even know the word. Freaked out, I guess. Because I want to spend every Christmas making meatballs with you."

"What about breaking tables?" He smirks, giving me a wink.

"That too."

"Good."

"But…but how?" I ask.

"I had Cary's number," he explains, answering my original question of how. It makes a light bulb go off, the memory of giving him Cary's number for the video call. It never occurred to me to ask if Cary still had saved the number from that. "He put me in touch with Brandt and Milo, who told me about the party."

"Oh. But I meant how, as in, you and me how. My life is here and yours is—"

"I can work anywhere. And my firm has an office in Atlanta. But, we don't have to figure that out now. Right now, all that matters to me is that you're in. Then we can determine the details."

"Of course I'm in!"

I launch myself at him, thankful that he catches me, pulling me in for a hot, hard kiss. Our tongues meet, and all the same fireworks from before ignite inside me, replacing the raw ache that had been there earlier. Forget everything else. This, right here, in Pierce's arms, is my happy place.

Setting me down, Pierce kisses me on the forehead, his lips leaving a searing mark, as if they have branded me. "I will want to spend a good amount of time here though. Brandt and I got to talking about distilling when I called them, and he's interested in some of the things that I've been trying with my gin."

I laugh, because, of course Brandt is. "We'll have to come up with a clever name for it then."

"Already have one. All Snowed Gin. Drew up a logo and everything—it has a rose on it."

I swoon, holding on to Pierce tighter. He could not be more perfect if he tried.

"All Snowed Gin. I love it."

"I love you, Rose. If it's not too bold of me to say."

"It's not," I sob, fresh tears spilling over. Happy tears. "Because I love you, Pierce."

"Y'all, it's almost midnight!" Willa's voice crackles over the loudspeaker. I smile brighter, since it seems her brother didn't find her. Maybe we'll both get happy endings tonight. "Ready? Ten…nine…"

The crowd counts down with her, but I don't turn to look. Instead, I stare into the eyes of my future, looking forward to the same happiness his grandparents had. As time winds down, the number getting smaller, Pierce smiles back at me.

"Happy New Year, Rose."

The clock strikes midnight and his lips are on mine, sealing this year as ours. This year, and every year to come.

Pierce and Rose spent this Christmas alone…but what about a Christmas with the whole family? One that includes something sparkly…

Download the All Snowed Gin Bonus Scene here!

THINKING 'BOUT YOU

CHAPTER 1

KENZIE

THE LARGE, brightly colored poster hangs on the glass entryway of the library like it's mocking me. Waving at me every time the door opens, or simply smirking at me knowingly when I look up from my desk. Either way, that stupid piece of cardstock knows what it's doing—I am convinced of it.

The fact that the top lefthand corner won't stay in place isn't helping.

I firmly press my thumb against the cardstock, willing it to adhere to the extra sticky tape I just replaced. For the third time this week. Yeah, definitely mocking me.

"So nice that Dustin Wild is coming back for the festival, isn't it?" says Mrs. Chamberlain, longtime math teacher and Hickory Hills native, pulling my attention back to the front desk where she is pushing a stack of books across the counter. "You must be excited to see him. A chance to reconnect."

Glancing at my watch, I wonder what she's doing here in the middle of a school day, but don't dare ask. Instead, I head toward the desk, rounding the corner quickly so I can get her out of here. Taking the stack of books, I scan them one by one, happy for an excuse not to make eye contact.

"You can't tell me you're not excited," she presses.

I don't need to look up to know there is a mischievous look on the older lady's face. I can hear it in her voice. She, along with most of our small Georgia town, is all abuzz about the return of Dustin Wild—or as we all knew him back then, Dustin Wilder—local boy turned country star, for our annual Rhythm and Brews Festival. Of course, her former student being a country star is not the reason that Mrs. Chamberlain is all atwitter in this moment. She's fishing for something—anything—to fuel the gossip mill. And I am not about to give it to her.

"If I even see him," I reply, forcing a smile. "I'll be so busy with everything that I doubt we'll have time for more than a quick hello."

There is a fine line between engaging the enemy and flat-out ignoring, and it's taken years of practice to find the proper balance. To know just how much information to give that will satisfy those curious, while not leaving room for speculation or giving up details you don't want to be made public. It's an art, really. One that only a lifetime in a small town teaches you. In my head, I picture Hickory Hills as the southern version of Stars Hollow. Small town, big charm, and unique personalities. Making Mrs. Chamberlain our equivalent of Miss Patty.

"Oh, I'm sure you will. You know, I always thought you two were going to go the distance. I've seen a lot of couples form over the years, and young love can be so fickle, but I usually have a good feel for who will and won't make it. You and Dustin, I would have put money on that."

And there it is.

Thanks, Mrs. Chamberlain...

I force my smile as big as I can, my cheeks starting to hurt from the pressure. "You're all set, Mrs. C. Just have these back no later than three weeks from Tuesday."

Opening her mouth to comment more, Mrs. Chamberlain snaps it shut just as quickly, realizing she isn't going to get anything else out of me. Continuing with my saccharine expression, I can see the thoughts pinging around her mind —it's fine that I'm being tight-lipped, because she's just going to send in reinforcements later. Too bad for her. I'm not going to be talking to them either.

I have nothing to say.

I have already said too much on the subject of Dustin. And *to* Dustin, nonetheless.

An incident that doesn't need repeating.

Because I, Kenzie Noble, am over Dustin Wilder.

Letting out a long sigh, I try to distract myself, returning to what I was doing before I stopped to deal with that mockingly obnoxious poster—sorting through the books that had been left in the return bin overnight. The summer reading program is in its last days, and if I'm doing my math right, we have a handful of kids who are closing in on their final goal. Success.

An outburst of giggles rings through the library, cutting through the silence. Without bothering to lift my gaze, I already know where it's coming from—I'd watched out of the corner of my eye as the group of tweens had walked in, casually heading for the thriller section, which was conveniently right next to romance. As if any tween girl was going to choose James Patterson over Nora Roberts.

Actually, that isn't fair. I know plenty of young women whose literary interests are firmly rooted in things other than romance, and their fervor for their genre of choice is always so much fun to witness. I also remember being that age, sneaking into the romance section with my two best friends, Willa Hayes and Sylvie Forde, searching out the books for the "good bits," giggling the whole time. Much like the giggles I'm hearing now. Of course, back then, old Mrs. Cassum, the former librarian, wasn't quite as understanding about interest in such subjects as I like to think I am.

No, I *know* I am.

The squeak of the door opening steals my attention, a reminder that I need to apply some WD-40 to the hinge. Add that to the never-ending to-do list. Looking up from the pile of books, I see Willa standing in the entrance, holding the door wide open, letting all the air conditioning escape as she stares at the poster.

"You're letting all the air out," I call out to her a few seconds later, apparently channeling my inner Mrs. Cassum. A sweep of warm August air whooshes toward me, notching up my annoyance.

"I still don't like what they did with the colors," Willa responds, turning to look at me, her nose crinkled in disgust. She pushes at the corner I just fixed, which is already starting to come loose again.

Maybe it's just time to take that damn thing down...

Stepping inside, Willa lets the door gently shut behind her, as she glides across the lobby. A former Miss Georgia, just like her mother, almost everything Willa does is graceful —even when she is cussing you out from both sides of her mouth, which, thanks to six older brothers, she's quite proficient at. Everyone in Hickory Hills knows what a spitfire Willa is—at least until she turns on the pageant queen, and then she becomes the epitome of southern charm.

"Take it up with Mrs. Burch. They're supposed to be veggies."

"Veggies? This is a barbecue festival. No one cares about veggies. She has been on this planet and lived in this town for six hundred years; she should know that."

I shrug, not sure how to counter that. Willa makes a

damn good point. Flicking my eyes back over to the poster and that damned corner, I read the words glaring back at me, even though at this point I can recite them.

Hickory Hills Annual Rhythm and Brews Festival
Presented by Southern Brothers Brewing and Hayes Industries
With special guest Dustin Wild
All proceeds benefit "A Noble Cause" to help fund Ken Noble's medical bills

"Ready for all this?" Willa asks.

"No," I answer tersely, picking up a stack of books and placing them on the return cart. "And not for the reason you think. But because I have five thousand and one things to do before thousands of people descend upon our itty-bitty town in search of barbecue and beer."

"And Dustin Wild."

And fucking Dustin Wild...

"Hey!" Sylvie shouts, walking into the library, hand flying over her mouth as she realizes how loud she is.

"Is this an intervention?" I ask, starting to worry about why they are both at the town library in the middle of the day. I can't remember the last time either of them stepped foot in here, unless expressly meeting me. Much less together.

"Is there a need for an intervention?" Willa asks.

Nope...because I'm not telling you my secret...

"We just wanted to see how you were," Sylvie offers.

The exact opposite to Willa's tall, leggy, and blonde, Sylvie is shorter, curvy, and has auburn hair that shimmers in the sunlight. The thick, black-framed glasses she sometimes wears are currently sliding down the bridge of her nose, making her look every ounce the science teacher she is. In some ways, these two women could not be any more different. But the three of us share a bond that can only come from a lifetime of friendship, and I wouldn't trade either of them for the world.

"Right…so we just took off in the middle of the day from teaching and whatever it is one does as the Director of Corporate Giving for a Fortune 500 company."

"We're on our lunch break," Willa answers, Sylvie nodding in agreement.

I don't believe either one of them and give them a look that lets them know that. For one, I know Sylvie has her hands full teaching physics, chemistry, and freshman physical science this year since they are shorthanded at the high school. Although, as the second teacher I've seen in here in the last twenty minutes, I'm starting to wonder what's going on at that school.

For two, it's Monday, which means Willa has "Munch," a weekly "meeting" where the head of every branch of Hayes Industries—otherwise known as her brothers, plus her and their father—have lunch together to talk about…again, whatever one talks about at that kind of thing. As the biggest employer in the area, tackling industries such as guns and ammo, agriculture, paper, personal safety, a brewery, and the local bait and tackle shop, there is no way the town librarian ends up on Hayes Industries' docket.

Nope. These two have an agenda.

"We just know you have a lot going on," Sylvie adds.

"No more than usual." I shrug, trying to brush it off, keeping my eye trained on the cart. Sure, this is going to be a heavy week, but it's nothing I can't handle.

"No more than usual," Willa scoffs. "Kenz, it's Rhythm and Brews week, which we all know means insanity. With everything you have to do to get ready for this thing, plus then actually execute it, on top of your regular job, that's a lot. Add in your dad having cancer and your sister being no help because she's a hundred and six weeks pregnant—"

"Thirty-six. Moira is only thirty-six weeks pregnant."

"Thirty-six, a hundred and six—whatever. She's no help to you either way."

I heave out a sigh, grateful they care but really wishing they would drop the issue. Releasing the wheel stoppers on the cart, I turn the corner around the front desk and head toward the fiction section. I can feel the two of them hot on my heels, not willing to let this go. Fine, then they can help me reshelve. They might be able to skip out on work, but I can't.

"I'm fine. Is it a lot of work? Yes. But it is every year. Also, I'm *on* the planning committee, I'm not the *whole* committee. And Dad is doing great." I stop, slipping a few books back into place before turning to face them. "Speaking of... Sylvie, I know I've asked before, but are you sure you don't mind that the money isn't going to the school? I still feel bad we hijacked your fundraiser."

"Yes! The town wants to rally around your dad. The robotics team will figure something out. Recycled parts? I don't know. Don't worry about it; it'll be a fun challenge."

I sigh, thankful again that my best friend doesn't care that her funding was pulled out from underneath her. It's not that I don't appreciate the gesture from the town—I do. And yes, we could use the money to pay for Dad's medical bills. But part of me still can't help feeling guilty.

"This is what small towns do," Willa reminds me. "Everyone has a Mr. Noble story. How many times a day does someone come in here and tell you a tale all about something your dad did for them or when he picked them up off the side of the road in his tow truck?"

I nod. She's right. Dad was born and raised here and has

always said Hickory Hills is in his blood. He's also just the kind of person who would do anything for anyone.

"Only about a dozen."

"Exactly."

"And then there's the other part," Sylvie says. "The tall, sandy-haired, megawatt smile, smooth as whiskey voice part."

"Why, thank you, I had forgotten for a brief second not only what he looks like, but what he sounds like."

I stomp off, annoyed at the reminder of my ex, pushing the cart as fast as I can through the stacks. Which isn't very fast. It's not an easy maneuver, but at least it's a distraction from him.

"Kenz."

Facing Dustin's return was inevitable, ever since Mrs. Burch announced at one of the festival planning meetings that she had reached out to him and his people, inviting him to come back for the event. That didn't mean I had to be happy about it.

"He and your dad were always so close, slaving away in that garage," she'd said, her fragile voice and deep southern accent making her sound as sweet as could be. "I figured he'd want to know about your dad's diagnosis and help out if he could. Sure enough, he's agreed."

The rest of the committee had been so excited, I didn't have the heart to speak up. I figured the questions would start soon enough—after all, the rumor mill hadn't stopped churning for years after he took off for Nashville, leaving me behind. When they didn't, well, I wasn't sure if I should be relieved or worried that it was all happening behind my back. Either way, I wasn't going to add any fuel to that fire.

"I know you still don't want to talk about it," Willa says. "But at some point, you have to. Preferably before he shows up."

I stop, whipping around to face them.

"What is there to talk about? My ex—who never actually ended things with me, but instead just left with the promise of returning and never did, and is now a freaking country star—is coming back to town to do a free show to raise money for my father. That's about all there is to it."

"When was the last time you spoke?"

A month ago. When I called him up, totally sober, completely out of the blue, just because I wanted to hear his voice. Because I missed him. *Miss* him.

"It's been a while," I lie. I can't tell them the truth. Not just because I didn't tell them then, but because no part of me wants to own up to what it might mean. That I'm not really over him. Which I am. Promise.

Except I might just be full of shit.

Silence hangs between us, the overhead lights bright enough to leave me feeling exposed, with even my best friends not knowing what else to say. They walked through all this with me as it happened and are here to support me now. I know they have my back no matter what this week throws at us. It's just too soon to tell what that might be.

"Okay, here's what we're gonna do," Willa declares, clapping her hands together. "Girls' night, tonight. Karaoke and dancing at The Giddy Up."

"No."

"Why? You have a hot date? You back with Jake and didn't tell us?"

"No, I am not back with Jake." Although "with" is a bit of an overstatement for the casualness that is my relationship with Jake Wright, manager of the local grocery.

"Then you're free to hang out with us. Blow off a little steam before R and B takes over our lives for the next few days."

Willa makes a damn good point. Again. One that I am having a harder and harder time arguing against.

"C'mon," Sylvie pleads. "It'll be fun. We can karaoke. We haven't done that since..." She trails off, a guilty look taking over. She suddenly remembers exactly the last time we did karaoke.

"The night we realized he wasn't coming back," I say, finishing off her sentence. "Five years ago. Which was two whole years after he left."

Sylvie nods slowly, eyes closed tightly. It's written all over her face that she can't believe she'd forgotten that part. Or that she'd brought it up now. I can't hold it against her. We've moved on. All of us.

"Right, well, I have to go. I'm late for Munch," Willa says, turning to make her exit. Stopping at the door, she sticks her tongue out at the poster, like she was six and it just tugged on her pigtails, before turning back and pointing at me. "I will pick you up at eight. You better have your boots on."

With a snap of her fingers she's gone, leaving Sylvie and me smiling at one another, waiting for the next round of giggles from the romance section.

Looks like I'm going dancing tonight.

WANT to know what happens when Dustin shows up? Keep reading THINKING 'BOUT YOU!

ALSO BY CLAIRE HASTINGS

Indigo Royal Resort

The Way You Make Me Feel

Can't Fight This Feeling

Caught Up In You

What I Like About You

Atlanta Rising Football Club

Game Time Decision

Out Of Bounds

Pressure Point

Offsides

Assist

Penalty Kick

Slide Tackle

Checking It Twice

Hickory Hills

Thinking 'Bout You

Workin' On You

Small Town Boy

Seein' Red

Adlers of Hickory Hills

Son of a Peach

All Snowed Gin

World of True North

Cakewalk

Stand Alone Novellas

A Novel Seduction

Hot Mess Christmas Express

ABOUT THE AUTHOR

USA TODAY Best Selling Author Claire Hastings is a walking, talking awkward moment. She loves Diet Coke, gummi bears, the beach, and books (obvs). When not reading she can usually be found hanging with friends at a soccer match or grabbing food (although she probably still has a book in her purse). She and her husband live in Atlanta.

She can be found here:

Instagram | Facebook | GoodReads | BookBub

You can sign up for her newsletter here.

Made in the USA
Middletown, DE
07 October 2024